Charlotte Riddell

Some Short Stories from the Queen of Irish Horror

British Library Cataloguing-in-Publication Data
A catalogue record for this book is available from
the British Library

Contents

Hertford O'Donnell's Warning.................1
Sandy the Tinker......................................23
The Old House in Vauxhall Walk.........36
The Banshee's Warning.........................55

A Biography of Charlotte Riddell.........77

HERTFORD O'DONNELL'S WARNING

Many a year, before chloroform was thought of, there lived in an old rambling house, in Gerrard Street, Soho, a clever Irishman called Hertford O'Donnell.

After Hertford O'Donnell he was entitled to write, MRCS for he had studied hard to gain this distinction, and the older surgeons at Guy's (his hospital) considered him one of the most rising operators of the day.

Having said chloroform was unknown at the time this story opens, it will strike my readers that, if Hertford O'Donnell were a rising and successful operator in those days, of necessity he combined within himself a larger number of striking qualities than are by any means necessary to form a successful operator in these.

There was more than mere hand skill, more than even thorough knowledge of his profession, then needful for the man, who, dealing with conscious subjects, essayed to rid them of some of the diseases to which flesh is heir. There was greater courage required in the manipulator or old than is altogether essential at present. Then, as now, a thorough mastery of his instruments, a steady hand, a keen eye, a quick dexterity were indispensable to a good operator; but, added to all these things, there formerly required a pulse which knew no quickening, a mental strength which never faltered, a ready power of adaptation in unexpected circumstances, fertility of resource in difficult cases, and a brave front under all emergencies.

If I refrain from adding that a hard as well as a courageous

1

heart was an important item in the programme, it is only out of deference to general opinion, which, amongst other strange delusions, clings to the belief that courage and hardness are antagonistic qualities.

Hertford O'Donnell, however, was hard as steel. He understood his work, and he did it thoroughly; but he cared no more for quivering nerves and shrinking muscles, for screams of agony, for faces white with pain, and teeth clenched in the extremity of anguish, than he did for the stony countenances of the dead, which so often in the dissecting room appalled younger and less experienced men.

He had no sentiment, and he had no sympathy. The human body was to him, merely an ingenious piece of mechanism, which it was at once a pleasure and a profit to understand. Precisely as Brunel loved the Thames Tunnel, or any other eingular engineering feat, so O'Donnell loved a patient on whom he had operated successfully, more especially if the ailment possessed by the patient were of a rare and difficult character.

And for this reason he was much liked by all who came under his hands, since patients are apt to mistake a surgeon's interest in their cases for interest in themselves; and it was gratifying to John Dicks, plasterer, and Timothy Regan, labourer, to be the happy possessors of remarkable diseases, which produced a cordial understanding between them and the handsome Irishman.

If he had been hard and cool at the moment of hacking them to pieces, that was all forgotten or remembered only as a virtue, when, after being discharged from hospital like soldiers who have served in a severe campaign, they met Mr O'Donnell in the street, and were accosted by that rising individual just as though he considered himself nobody.

He had a royal memory, this stranger in a strange land, both for faces and cases; and like the rest of his countrymen, he never felt it beneath his dignity to talk cordially to corduroy and fustian.

In London, as a Calgillan, he never held back his tongue from speaking a cheery or a kindly word. His manners were pliable enough, if his heart were not; and the porters, and the patients, and the nurses, and the students at Guy's were all pleased to see Hertford O'Donnell.

Rain, hail, sunshine, it was all the same; there was a life and a brightness about the man which communicated itself to those with whom he came in contact. Let the mud in the Borough be a foot deep or the London fog as thick as pea-soup, Mr O'Donnell never lost his temper, never muttered a surly reply to the gatekeeper's salutation, but spoke out blithely and cheerfully to his pupils and his patients, to the sick and to the well, to those below and to those above him.

And yet, spite of all these good qualities, spite of his handsome face, his fine figure, his easy address, and his unquestionable skill as an operator, the dons, who acknowledged his talent, shook their heads gravely when two or three of them in private and solemn conclave, talked confidentially of their younger brother.

If there were many things in his favour, there were more in his disfavour. He was Irish—not merely by the accident of birth, which might have been forgiven, since a man cannot be held accountable for such caprices of Nature, but by every other accident and design which is objectionable to the orthodox and respectable and representative English mind.

In speech, appearance, manner, taste, modes of expression, habits of life, Hertford O'Donnell was Irish. To the core of his heart he loved the island which he declared he never meant to re-visit; and amongst the English he moved to all intents and purposes a foreigner, who was resolved, so said the great prophets at Guy's, to rush to destruction as fast as he could, and let no man hinder him.

'He means to go the whole length of his tether,' observed one of the ancient wiseacres to another; which speech implied a conviction that Hertford O'Donnell having sold himself to the Evil One, had determined to dive the full length of his rope into wickedness before being pulled to

3

that shore where even wickedness is negative—where there are no mad carouses, no wild, sinful excitements, nothing but impotent wailing and gnashing of teeth.

A reckless, graceless, clever, wicked devil—going to his natural home as fast as in London anyone possibly speed thither; this was the opinion his superiors, held of the man who lived all alone with a housekeeper and her husband (who acted as butler) in his big house near Soho.

Gerrard Street—made famous by De Quincey, was not then an utterly shady and forgotten locality; carriage-patients found their way to the rising young surgeon—some great personages thought it not beneath them to fee an individual whose consulting rooms were situated on what was even then considered the wrong side of Regent Street. He was making money, and he was spending it; he was over head and ears in debt—useless, vulgar debt—senselessly contracted, never bravely faced. He had lived at an awful pace ever since he came to London, a pace which only a man who hopes and expects to die young can ever travel.

Life was good, was it? Death, was he a child, or a woman, or a coward, to be afraid of that hereafter? God knew all about the trifle which had upset his coach, better than the dons at Guy's.

Hertford O'Donnell understood the world pretty thoroughly, and the ways thereof were to him as roads often traversed; therefore, when he said that at the Day of Judgment he felt certain he should come off as well as many of those who censured him, it may be assumed, that, although his views of post-mortem punishment were vague, unsatisfactory and infidel, still his information as to the peccadilloes of his neighbours was such as consoled himself.

And yet, living all alone in the old house near Soho Square, grave thoughts would intrude into the surgeon's mind—thoughts which were, so to say, italicised by peremptory letters, and still more peremptory visits from people who wanted money.

Although he had many acquaintances he had no single

4

friend, and accordingly these thoughts were received and brooded over in solitude—in those hours when, after returning from dinner, or supper, or congenial carouse, he sat in his dreary rooms, smoking his pipe and considering means and ways, chances and certainties.

In good truth he had started in London with some vague idea that as his life in it would not be of long continuance, the pace at which he elected to travel could be of little consequence; but the years since his first entry into the Metropolis were now piled one on the top of another, his youth was behind him, his chances of longevity, spite of the way he had striven to injure his constitution, quite as good as ever. He had come to that period in existence, to that narrow strip of tableland, whence the ascent of youth and the descent of age are equally discernible—when, simply because he has lived for so many years, it strikes a man as possible he may have to live for just as many more, with the ability for hard work gone, with the boom companions scattered, with the capacity for enjoying convivial meetings a mere memory, with small means perhaps, with no bright hopes, with the pomp and the circumstance and the fairy carriages, and the glamour which youth flings over earthly objects, faded away like the pageant of yesterday, while the dreary ceremony of living has to be gone through today and tomorrow and the morrow after, as though the gay cavalcade and the martial music, and the glittering helmets and the prancing steeds were still accompanying the wayfarer to his journey's end.

Ah! my friends, there comes a moment when we must all leave the coach, with its four bright bays, its pleasant outside freight, its cheery company, its guard who blows the horn so merrily through villages and along lonely country roads.

Long before we reach that final stage, where the black business claims us for its own special property, we have to bid goodbye to all easy, thoughtless journeying, and betake ourselves, with what zest we may, to traversing the common of reality. There is no royal road across it that ever I heard of. From the king on his throne to the labourer who vaguely imagines what manner of being a king is, we have all to tramp across that desert at one period of our lives, at all events; and that period usually is when, as I have said, a man starts to find the hopes, and the strength, and the buoyancy of youth left behind, while years and years of life lie stretching out before him.

The coach he has travelled by drops him here. There is no appeal, there is no help; therefore, let him take off his hat and wish the new passengers good speed, without either envy or repining.

Behold, he has had his turn, and let whosoever will, mount on the box-seat of life again, and tip the coachman and handle the ribbons—he shall take that pleasant journey no more, no more for ever.

Even supposing a man's springtime to have been a cold and ungenial one, with bitter easterly winds and nipping frosts, biting the buds and retarding the blossoms, still it was spring for all that—spring with the young green leaves sprouting forth, with the flowers unfolding tenderly, with the songs of the birds and the rush of waters, with the summer before and the autumn afar off, and winter remote as death and eternity, but when once the trees have donned their summer foliage, when the pure white blossoms have disappeared, and the gorgeous red and orange and purple blaze of many-coloured flowers fills the gardens, then if there come a wet, dreary day, the idea of autumn and winter is not so difficult to realise. When once twelve o'clock is reached, the evening and night become facts, not possibilities; and it was of the afternoon, and the evening, and the night, Hertford O'Donnell sat thinking on the Christmas Eve, when I crave permission to introduce him to my readers.

A good-looking man ladies considered him. A tall, dark-complexioned, black-haired, straight-limbed, deeply divinely blue-eyed fellow, with a soft voice, with a pleasant brogue, who had ridden like a centaur over the loose stone walls in Connemara, who had danced all night at the Dublin balls, who had walked across the Bennebeola Mountains, gun in hand, day after day, without weariness, who had fished in every one of the hundred lakes you can behold from the top of that mountain near the Recess Hotel, who had led a mad, wild life in Trinity College, and a wilder, perhaps, while 'studying for a doctor'—as the Irish phrase goes—in Edinburgh, and who, after the death of his eldest brother left him free to return to Calgillan, and pursue the usual utterly useless, utterly purposeless, utterly pleasant life of an Irish gentleman possessed of health, birth, and expectations, suddenly kicked over the paternal traces, bade adieu to Calgillan Castle and the blandishments of a certain beautiful Miss Clifden, beloved of his mother, and laid out to be his wife, walked down the avenue without even so much company as a Gossoon to carry his carpet-bag, shook the dust from his feet at the lodge gates, and took his seat on the coach, never once looking back at Calgillan, where his favourite mare was standing in the stable, his greyhounds chasing one another round the home paddock, his gun at half-cock in his dressing-room and his fishing-tackle all in order and ready for use.

He had not kissed his mother, or asked for his father's blessing; he left Miss Clifden, arrayed in her brand-new riding-habit, without a word of affection or regret; he had spoken no syllable of farewell to any servant about the place; only when the old woman at the lodge bade him good morning and God-blessed his handsome face, he recommended her bitterly to look at it well for she would never see it more.

Twelve years and a half had passed since then, without either Miss Clifden or any other one of the Calgillan people having set eyes on Master Hertford's handsome face.

He had kept his vow to himself; he had not written home; he had not been indebted to mother or father for even a tenpenny-piece during the whole of that time; he had lived without friends; and he had lived without God—so far as God ever lets a man live without him.

One thing only he felt to be needful—money; money to

keep him when the evil days of sickness, or age, or loss of practice came upon him. Though a spendthrift, he was not a simpleton; around him he saw men, who, having started with fairer prospects than his own, were, nevertheless, reduced to indigence; and he knew that what had happened to others might happen to himself.

An unlucky cut, slipping on a piece of orange-peel in the street, the merest accident imaginable, is sufficient to change opulence to beggary in the life's programme of an individual, whose income depends on eye, on nerve, on hand; and, besides the consciousness of this fact, Hertford O'Donnell knew that beyond a certain point in his profession, progress was not easy.

It did not depend quite on the strength of his own bow and shield whether he counted his earnings by hundreds or thousands. Work may achieve competence; but mere work cannot, in a profession, at all events, compass fortune.

He looked around him, and he perceived that the majority of great men—great and wealthy—had been indebted for their elevation, more to the accident of birth, patronage, connection, or marriage, than to personal ability.

Personal ability, no doubt, they possessed; but then, little Jones, who lived in Frith Street, and who could barely keep himself and his wife and family, had ability, too, only he lacked the concomitants of success.

He wanted something or someone to puff him into notoriety—a brother at Court—a lord's leg to mend—a rich wife to give him prestige in Society; and in his absence of this something or someone, he had grown grey-haired and faint-hearted while labouring for a world which utterly despises its most obsequious servants.

'Clatter along the streets with a pair of fine horses, snub the middle classes, and drive over the commonalty—that is the way to compass wealth and popularity in England,' said Hertford O'Donnell, bitterly; and as the man desired wealth and popularity, he sat before his fire, with a foot on each hob, and a short pipe in his mouth, considering how he might best obtain the means to clatter along the streets in his carriage, and splash plebeians with mud from his wheels like the best.

In Dublin he could, by means of his name and connection, have done well; but then he was not in Dublin, neither did he want to be. The bitterest memories of his life were inseparable from the very name of the Green Island, and he had no desire to return to it.

Besides, in Dublin, heiresses are not quite so plentiful as in London; and an heiress, Hertford O'Donnell had decided, would do more for him than years of steady work.

A rich wife could clear him of debt, introduce him to fashionable practice, afford him that measure of social respectability which a medical bachelor invariably lacks, deliver him from the loneliness of Gerrard Street, and the domination of Mr and Mrs Coles.

To most men, deliberately bartering away their independence for money seems so prosaic a business that they strive to gloss it over even to themselves, and to assign every reason for their choice, save that which is really the influencing one.

Not so, however, with Hertford O'Donnell. He sat beside the fire scoffing over his proposed bargain—thinking of the lady's age, her money bags, her desirable house in town, her seat in the country, her snobbishness, her folly.

'It could be a fitting ending,' he sneered, 'and why I did not settle the matter tonight passes my comprehension. I am not a fool, to be frightened with old women's tales; and yet I must have turned white. I felt I did, and she asked me whether I were ill. And then to think of my being such an idiot as to ask her if she had heard anything like a cry, as though she would be likely to hear *that*, she with her poor parvenu blood, which I often imagine must have been mixed with some of her father's strong pickling vinegar. What a deuce could I have been dreaming about? I wonder what it really was.' And Hertford O'Donnell pushed his hair back off his forehead, and took another draught from the too

9

familiar tumbler, which was placed conveniently on the chimney-piece.

'After expressly making up my mind to propose, too!' he mentally continued. 'Could it have been conscience—that myth, which somebody, who knew nothing about the matter, said, "Makes cowards of us all"? I don't believe in conscience; and even if there be such a thing capable of being developed by sentiment and cultivation, why should it trouble me? I have no intention of wronging Miss Janice Price Ingot, not the least. Honestly and fairly I shall marry her; honestly and fairly I shall act by her. An old wife is not exactly an ornamental article of furniture in a man's house; and I do not know that the fact of her being well gilded makes her look any handsomer. But she shall have no cause for complaint; and I will go and dine with her tomorrow, and settle the matter.'

Having arrived at which resolution, Mr O'Donnell arose, kicked down the fire—burning hollow—with the heel of his boot, knocked the ashes out of his pipe, emptied his tumbler, and bethought him it was time to go to bed. He was not in the habit of taking his rest so early as a quarter to twelve o'clock; but he felt unusually weary—tired mentally and bodily—and lonely beyond all power of expression.

'The fair Janet would be better than this,' he said, half aloud; and then, with a start and a shiver, and a blanched face, he turned sharply round, whilst a low, sobbing, wailing cry echoed mournfully through the room. No form of words could give an idea of the sound. The plaintiveness of the Æolian harp—that plaintiveness which so soon affects and lowers the highest spirits—would have seemed wildly gay in comparison with the sadness of the cry which seemed floating in the air. As the summer wind comes and goes amongst the trees, so that mournful wail came and went—came and went. It came in a rush of sound, like a gradual crescendo managed by a skilful musician, and died away in a lingering note, so gently that the listener could scarcely tell the exact moment when it faded into utter silence.

I say faded, for it disappeared as the coast line disappears in the twilight, and there was total stillness in the apartment.

Then, for the first time, Hertford O'Donnell looked at his dog, and beholding the creature crouched into a corner beside the fireplace, called upon him to come out.

His voice sounded strange even to himself, and apparently the dog thought so too, for he made no effort to obey the summons.

'Come here, sir,' his master repeated, and then the animal came crawling reluctantly forward with his hair on end, his eyes almost starting from his head, trembling violently, as the surgeon, who caressed him, felt.

'So you heard it, Brian?' he said to the dog. 'And so your· ears are sharper than Miss Ingot's, old fellow. It's a mighty queer thing to think of, being favoured with a visit from a Banshee in Gerrard Street; and as the lady has travelled so far, I only wish I knew whether there is any sort of refreshment she would like to take after her long journey.'

He spoke loudly, and with a certain mocking defiance, seeming to think the phantom he addressed would reply; but when he stopped at the end of his sentence, no sound came through the stillness. There was a dead silence in the room —a silence broken only by the falling of cinders on the hearth and the breathing of his dog.

'If my visitor would tell me,' he proceeded, 'for whom this lamentation is being made, whether for myself, or for some member of my illustrious family, I should feel immensely obliged. It seems too much honour for a poor surgeon to have such attention paid him. Good Heavens! What is that?' he exclaimed, as a ring, loud and peremptory, woke all the echoes in the house, and brought his house-keeper, in a state of distressing dishabille, 'out of her warm bed', as she subsequently stated, to the head of the staircase.

Across the hall Hertford O'Donnell strode, relieved at the prospect of speaking to any living being. He took no precaution of putting up the chain, but flung the door wide. A dozen burglars would have proved welcome in comparison

11

with that ghostly intruder he had been interviewing; therefore, as has been said, he threw the door wide, admitting a rush of wet, cold air, which made poor Mrs Coles' few remaining teeth chatter in her head.

'Who is there? What do you want?' asked the surgeon, seeing no person, and hearing no voice. 'Who is there? Why the devil can't you speak?'

When even this polite exhortation failed to elicit an answer, he passed out into the night and looked up the street and down the street, to see nothing but the driving rain and the blinking lights.

'If this goes on much longer I shall soon think I must be either mad or drunk,' he muttered, as he re-entered the house and locked and bolted the door once more.

'Lord's sake! What is the matter, sir?' asked Mrs Coles, from the upper flight, careful only to reveal the borders of her night-cap to Mr O'Donnell's admiring gaze. 'Is anybody killed? Have you to go out, sir?'

'It was only a run-away ring,' he answered, trying to reassure himself with an explanation he did not in his heart believe.

'Run-away—I'd run away them!' murmured Mrs Coles, as she retired to the conjugal couch, where Coles was, to quote her own expression, 'snoring like a pig through it all'.

Almost immediately afterwards she heard her master ascend the stairs and close his bedroom door.

'Madam will surely be too much of a gentlewoman to intrude here,' thought the surgeon, scoffing even at his own fears; but when he lay down he did not put out his light, and made Brian leap up and crouch on the coverlet beside him.

The man was fairly frightened, and would have thought it no discredit to his manhood to acknowledge as much. He was not afraid of death, he was not afraid of trouble, he was not afraid of danger; but he was afraid of the Banshee; and as he lay with his hand on the dog's head, he recalled the many stories he had been told concerning this family retainer in the days of his youth.

He had not thought about her for years and years. Never before had he heard her voice himself. When his brother died she had not thought it necessary to travel up to Dublin and give him notice of the impending catastrophe. 'If she had, I would have gone down to Calgillan, and perhaps saved his life,' considered the surgeon. 'I wonder who this is for? If for me, that will settle my debts and my marriage. If I could be quite certain it was either of the old people, I would start tomorrow.'

Then vaguely his mind wandered on to think of every Banshee story he had ever heard in his life. About the beautiful lady with the wreath of flowers, who sat on the rocks below Red Castle, in the County Antrim, crying till one of the sons died for love of her; about the Round Chamber at Dunluce, which was swept clean by the Banshee every night; about the bed in a certain great house in Ireland, which was slept in constantly, although no human being ever passed in or out after dark; about that General Officer who, the night before Waterloo, said to a friend, 'I have heard the Banshee, and shall not come off the field alive tomorrow; break the news gently to poor Carry'; and who, nevertheless, coming safe off the field, had subsequently news about poor Carry broken tenderly and pitifully to him; about the lad, who, aloft in the rigging, hearing through the night a sobbing and wailing coming over the waters, went down to the captain and told him he was afraid they were somehow out of their reckoning, just in time to save the ship, which, when morning broke, they found but for his warning would have been on the rocks. It was blowing great guns, and the sea was all in a fret and turmoil, and they could sometimes see in the trough of the waves, as down a valley, thè cruel black reefs they had escaped.

On deck the captain stood speaking to the boy who had saved them, and asking how he knew of their danger; and when the lad told him, the captain laughed, and said her ladyship had been outwitted that time.

But the boy answered, with a grave shake of his head,

that the warning was either for him or his, and that if he got safe to port there would be bad tidings waiting for him from home; whereupon the captain bade him go below, and get some brandy and lie down.

He got the brandy, and he lay down, but he never rose again; and when the storm abated—when a great calm succeeded to the previous tempest—there was a very solemn funeral at sea; and on their arrival at Liverpool the captain took a journey to Ireland to tell a widowed mother how her only son died, and to bear his few effects to the poor desolate soul.

And Hertford O'Donnell thought again about his own father riding full-chase across country, and hearing, as he galloped by a clump of plantation, something like a sobbing and wailing. The hounds were in full cry, but he still felt, as he afterwards expressed it, that there was something among those trees he could not pass; and so he jumped off his horse, and hung the reins over the branch of a Scotch fir, and beat the cover well, but not a thing could he find in it.

Then, for the first time in his life, Miles O'Donnell turned his horse's head *from* the hunt, and, within a mile of Calgillan, met a man running to tell him his brother's gun had burst, and injured him mortally.

And he remembered the story also, of how Mary O'Donnell, his great aunt, being married to a young Englishman, heard the Banshee as she sat one evening waiting for his return; and of how she, thinking the bridge by which he often came home unsafe for horse and man, went out in a great panic, to meet and entreat him to go round by the main road for her sake. Sir Edward was riding along in the moonlight, making straight for the bridge, when he beheld a figure dressed all in white crossing it. Then there was a crash, and the figure disappeared.

The lady was rescued and brought back to the hall; but next morning there were two dead bodies within its walls—those of Lady Eyreton and her still-born son.

Quicker than I write them, these memories chased one

another through Hertford O'Donnell's brain; and there was one more terrible memory than any, which would recur to him, concerning an Irish nobleman who, seated alone in his great town-house in London, heard the Banshee, and rushed out to get rid of the phantom, which wailed in his ear, nevertheless, as he strode down Piccadilly. And then the surgeon remembered how that nobleman went with a friend to the Opera, feeling sure that there no Banshee, unless she had a box, could find admittance, until suddenly he heard her singing up amongst the highest part of the scenery, with a terrible mournfulness, and a pathos which made the prima donna's tenderest notes seem harsh by comparison.

As he came out, some quarrel arose between him and a famous fire-eater, against whom he stumbled; and the result was that the next afternoon there was a new Lord, for he was killed in a duel with Captain Bravo.

Memories like these are not the most enlivening possible; they are apt to make a man fanciful, and nervous, and wakeful; but as time ran on, Hertford O'Donnell fell asleep, with his candle still burning, and Brian's cold nose pressed against his hand.

He dreamt of his mother's family—the Hertfords of Artingbury, Yorkshire, far-off relatives of Lord Hertford—so far off that even Mrs O'Donnell held no clue to the genealogical maze.

He thought he was at Artingbury, fishing; that it was a misty summer morning, and the fish rising beautifully. In his dreams he hooked one after another, and the boy who was with him threw them into the basket.

At last there was one more difficult to land than the others; and the boy, in his eagerness to watch the sport, drew nearer and nearer to the brink, while the fisher, intent on his prey, failed to notice his companion's danger.

Suddenly there was a cry, a splash, and the boy disappeared from sight.

Next instance he rose again, however, and then, for the first time, Hertford O'Donnell saw his face.

It was one he knew well.

In a moment he plunged into the water, and struck out for the lad. He had him by the hair, he was turning to bring him back to land, when the stream suddenly changed into a wide, wild, shoreless sea, where the billows were chasing one another with a mad demoniac mirth.

For a while O'Donnell kept the lad and himself afloat. They were swept under the waves, and came up again, only to see larger waves rushing towards them; but through all, the surgeon never loosened his hold, until a tremendous billow, engulfing them both, tore the boy from his grasp.

With the horror of his dream upon him he awoke, to hear a voice quite distinctly:

'Go to the hospital—go at once!'

The surgeon started up in bed, rubbing his eyes, and looked around. The candle was flickering faintly in its socket. Brian, with his ears pricked forward, had raised his head at his master's sudden movement.

Everything was quiet, but still those words were ringing in his ear:

'Go to the hospital—go at once!'

The tremendous peal of the bell over night, and this sentence, seemed to be simultaneous.

That he was wanted at Guy's—wanted imperatively—came to O'Donnell like an inspiration. Neither sense nor reason had anything to do with the conviction that roused him out of bed, and made him dress as speedily as possible, and grope his way down the staircase, Brian following.

He opened the front door, and passed out into the darkness. The rain was over, and the stars were shining as he pursued his way down Newport Market, and thence, winding in and out in a south-easterly direction, through Lincoln's Inn Fields and Old Square to Chancery Lane, whence he proceeded to St Paul's.

Along the deserted streets he resolutely continued his walk. He did not know what he was going to Guy's for. Some instinct was urging him on, and he neither strove to combat nor control it. Only once did the thought of turning back cross his mind, and that was the archway leading into Old Square. There he had paused for a moment, asking himself whether he were not gone stark, staring mad; but Guy's seemed preferable to the haunted house in Gerrard Street, and he walked resolutely on, determined to say, if any surprise were expressed at his appearance, that he had been sent for.

Sent for?—yea, truly; but by whom?

On through Cannon Street; on over London Bridge, where the lights flickered in the river, and the sullen splash of the water flowing beneath the arches, washing the stone piers, could be heard, now the human din was hushed and lulled to sleep. On, thinking of many things: of the days of his youth; of his dead brother; of his father's heavily-encumbered estate; of the fortune his mother had vowed she would leave to some charity rather than to him, if he refused to marry according to her choice; of his wild life in London; of the terrible cry he had heard over-night—that unearthly wail which he could not drive from his memory even when he entered Guy's, and confronted the porter, who said:

'You have been sent for, sir; did you meet the messenger?'

Like one in a dream, Hertford O'Donnell heard him; like one in a dream, also, he asked what was the matter.

'Bad accident, sir; fire; fell off a balcony—unsafe—old building. Mother and child—a son; child with compound fracture of thigh.'

This, the joint information of porter and house-surgeon, mingled together, and made a boom in Mr O'Donnell's ears like the sound of the sea breaking on a shingly shore.

Only one sentence he understood properly—'Immediate amputation necessary.' At this point he grew cool; he was the careful, cautious, successful surgeon, in a moment.

'The child you say?' he answered. 'Let me see him.'

The Guy's Hospital of today may be different to the Guy's Hertford O'Donnell knew so well. Railways have, I believe, swept away the old operating room; railways may have changed the position of the former accident ward, to reach which, in the days of which I am writing, the two surgeons had to pass a staircase leading to the upper stories.

On the lower step of this staircase, partially in shadow, Hertford O'Donnell beheld, as he came forward, an old woman seated.

An old woman with streaming grey hair, with attenuated arms, with head bowed forward, with scanty clothing, with bare feet; who never looked up at their approach, but sat unnoticing, shaking her head and wringing her hands in an extremity of despair.

'Who is that?' asked Mr O'Donnell, almost involuntarily.

'Who is what?' demanded his companion.

'That—that woman,' was the reply.

'What woman?'

'There—are you blind?—seated on the bottom step of the staircase. What is she doing?' persisted Mr O'Donnell.

'There is no woman near us,' his companion answered, looking at the rising surgeon very much as though he suspected him of seeing double.

'No woman!' scoffed Hertford. 'Do you expect me to disbelieve the evidence of my own eyes?' and he walked up to the figure, meaning to touch it.

But as he assayed to do so, the woman seemed to rise in the air and float away, with her arms stretched high up-over her head, uttering such a wail of pain, and agony, and distress, as caused the Irishman's blood to curdle.

'My God! Did you hear that?' he said to his companion.

'What?' was the reply.

Then, although he knew the sound had fallen on deaf ears, he answered:

'The wail of the Banshee! Some of my people are doomed!'

'I trust not,' answered the house-surgeon, who had an idea, nevertheless, that Hertford O'Donnell's Banshee lived in a whisky bottle, and would at some remote day make an end to the rising and clever operator.

With nerves utterly shaken, Mr O'Donnell walked forward to the accident ward. There with his face shaded from the light, lay his patient—a young boy, with a compound fracture of the thigh.

In that ward, in the face of actual danger or pain capable of relief the surgeon had never known faltering or fear; and now he carefully examined the injury, felt the pulse, inquired as to the treatment pursued, and ordered the sufferer to be carried to the operating room.

While he was looking out his instruments he heard the boy lying on the table murmur faintly:

'Tell her not to cry so—tell her not to cry.'

'What is he talking about?' Hertford O'Donnell inquired.

'The nurse says he has been speaking about some woman crying ever since he came in—his mother, most likely,' answered one of the attendants.

'He is delirious then?' observed the surgeon.

'No, sir,' pleaded the boy, excitedly, 'no; it is that woman —that woman with the grey hair. I saw her looking from the upper window before the balcony gave way. She has never left me since, and she won't be quiet, wringing her hands and crying.'

'Can you see her now?' Hertford O'Donnell inquired, stepping to the side of the table. 'Point out where she is.'

Then the lad stretched forth a feeble finger in the direction of the door, where clearly, as he had seen her seated on the stairs, the surgeon saw a woman standing—a woman with grey hair and scanty clothing, and upstretched arms and bare feet.

'A word with you, sir,' O'Donnell said to the house-surgeon, drawing him back from the table. 'I cannot perform this operation: send for some other person. I am ill; I am incapable.'

'But,' pleaded the other, 'there is no time to get anyone else. We sent for Mr West, before we troubled you, but he was out of town, and all the rest of the surgeons live so far away. Mortification may set in at any moment and—'.

'Do you think you require to teach me my business?' was the reply. 'I know the boy's life hangs on a thread, and that is the very reason I cannot operate. I am not fit for it. I tell you I have seen tonight that which unnerves me utterly. My hand is not steady. Send for someone else without delay. Say I am ill—dead!—what you please. Heavens! There she is again, right over the boy! Do you hear her?' and Hertford O'Donnell fell fainting on the floor.

How long he lay in that death-like swoon I cannot say; but when he returned to consciousness, the principal physician of Guy's was standing beside him in the cold grey light of the Christmas morning.

'The boy?' murmured O'Donnell, faintly.

'Now, my dear fellow, keep yourself quiet,' was the reply.

'The boy?' he repeated, irritably. 'Who operated?'

'No one,' Dr Lanson answered. 'It would have been useless cruelty. Mortification had set in and—'

Hertford O'Donnell turned his face to the wall, and his friend could not see it.

'Do not distress yourself,' went on the physician, kindly. 'Allington says he could not have survived the operation in any case. He was quite delirious from the first, raving about a woman with grey hair and—'

'I know,' Hertford O'Donnell interrupted; 'and the boy had a mother, they told me, or I dreamt it.'

'Yes, she was bruised and shaken, but not seriously injured.'

'Has she blue eyes and fair hair—fair hair all rippling and wavy? Is she white as a lily, with just a faint flush of colour in her cheek? Is she young and trusting and innocent? No; I am wandering. She must be nearly thirty now. Go, for God's sake, and tell me if you can find a woman you could imagine having once been as a girl such as I describe.'

'Irish?' asked the doctor; and O'Donnell made a gesture of assent.

'It is she then,' was the reply, 'a woman with the face of an angel.'

'A woman who should have been my wife,' the surgeon answered; 'whose child was my son.'

'Lord help you!' ejaculated the doctor. Then Hertford O'Donnell raised himself from the sofa where they had laid him, and told his companion the story of his life—how there had been bitter feud between his people and her people—how they were divided by old animosities and by difference of religion—how they had met by stealth, and exchanged rings and vows, all for naught—how his family had insulted hers, so that her father, wishful for her to marry a kinsman of his own, bore her off to a far-away land, and made her write him a letter of eternal farewell—how his own parents had kept all knowledge of the quarrel from him till she was utterly beyond his reach—how they had vowed to discard him unless he agreed to marry according to their wishes—how he left home, and came to London, and sought his fortune. All this Hertford O'Donnell repeated; and when he had finished, the bells were ringing for morning service—ringing loudly, ringing joyfully, 'Peace on earth, goodwill towards men'.

But there was little peace that morning for Hertford O'Donnell. He had to look on the face of his dead son, wherein he beheld, as though reflected, the face of the boy in his dream.

Afterwards, stealthily he followed his friend, and beheld, with her eyes closed, her cheeks pale and pinched, her hair thinner but still falling like a veil over her, the love of his youth, the only woman he had ever loved devotedly and unselfishly.

There is little space left here to tell of how the two met at last—of how the stone of the years seemed suddenly rolled away from the tomb of their past, and their youth arose and returned to them, even amid their tears.

She had been true to him, through persecution, through contumely, through kindness, which was more trying; through shame, and grief, and poverty, she had been loyal to the lover of her youth; and before the New Year dawned there came a letter from Calgillan, saying that the Banshee's wail had been heard there, and praying Hertford, if he were still alive, to let bygones be bygones, in consideration of the long years of estrangement—the anguish and remorse of his afflicted parents.

More than that. Hertford O'Donnell, if a reckless man, was honourable; and so, on the Christmas Day when he was to have proposed for Miss Ingot, he went to that lady, and told her how he had wooed and won, in the years of his youth, one who after many days was miraculously restored to him; and from the hour in which he took her into his confidence, he never thought her either vulgar or foolish, but rather he paid homage to the woman who, when she had heard the whole tale repeated, said, simply, 'Ask her to come to me till you can claim her—and God bless you both!'

SANDY THE TINKER

"Before commencing my story, I wish to state it is perfectly true in every particular."

"We quite understand that," said the sceptic of our party, who was wont, in the security of friendly intercourse, to characterise all such prefaces as mere introductions to some tremendously exaggerated tale.

On the occasion in question, however, we had donned our best behaviour, a garment which did not sit ungracefully on some of us; and our host, who was about to draw out from the stores of memory one narrative for our entertainment, was scarcely the person before whom even Jack Hill, the sceptic, would have cared to express his cynical and unbelieving views.

We were seated, an incongruous company of ten persons, in the best room of an old manse among the Scottish hills. Accident had thrown us together, and accident had driven us under the minister's hospitable roof. Cold, wet and hungry, drenched with rain, sorely beaten by the wind, we had crowded through the door opened by a friendly hand, and now, wet no longer, the pangs of hunger assuaged with smoking rashers of ham, poached eggs, and steaming potatoes, we sat around a blazing fire, drinking toddy out of tumblers, whilst the two ladies who graced the assemblage partook of a modicum of the same beverage from wine glasses.

Everything was eminently comfortable, but conducted upon the most correct principles. Jack could no more have taken it upon himself to shock the minister's ear with some of the opinions he aired in Fleet Street, than he could have asked for more whisky with his water.

"Yes, it is perfectly true," continued the minister, looking thoughtfully at the fire. "I can't explain it, I cannot even try to explain it. I will tell you the story exactly as it occurred, however, and leave you to draw your own deductions from it."

None of us answered. We fell into listening attitudes instantly, and eighteen eyes fixed themselves by one accord upon our host.

He was an old man, but hale. The weight of eighty winters had whitened his head, but not bowed it. He seemed young as any of us —younger than Jack Hill, who was a reviewer and a newspaper hack, and whose way through life had not been altogether on easy lines.

"Thirty years ago, upon a certain Friday morning in August," began the minister, "I was sitting at breakfast in the room on the other side of the passage, where you ate your supper, when the servant girl came in with a letter. She said a laddie, all out of breath, had brought it over from Dendeldy Manse. "He was bidden to rin a' the way," she went on, "and he's fairly beaten."

'I told her to make the messenger sit down, and put food before him; and then, when she went to do my bidding, proceeded, I must confess with some curiosity, to break the seal of a missive forwarded in such hot haste.

"It was from the minister at Dendeldy, who had been newly chosen to occupy the pulpit his deceased father occupied for a quarter of a century and more.

"The call from the congregation originated rather out of respect to the father's memory than any extraordinary liking for the son. He had been reared for the most part in England, and was somewhat distant and formal in his manners; and, though full of Greek and Latin and Hebrew, wanted the true Scotch accent, that goes straight to the heart of those accustomed to the broad, honest, tender Scottish tongue.

"His people were proud of him, but they did not like some of his ways. They could remember him a lad running about the whole country-side, and they could not understand, and did not approve of his holding them at arm's length, and shutting himself up among his books and refusing their hospitality, and sending out word he was busy when maybe some very decent man wanted speech with him. I had taken it upon myself to point out that I thought he was wrong, and that he would alienate his flock from him. Perhaps it was for this very reason, because I was blunt and plain, he took to me kindly, and never got on his high horse, no matter what I said to him.

"Well, to return to the letter. It was written in the wildest haste, and entreated me not to lose a moment in coming to him, as he was in the very *greatest distress* and *anxiety*. 'Let *nothing* delay you,' he proceeded. 'If I cannot speak to you soon I believe I shall go out of my senses.'

"What could be the matter? I thought. What in all the wide earth could have happened?

"I had seen him but a few days before and he was in good health and spirits, getting on better with his people, feeling hopeful of so altering his style of preaching as to touch their hearts more sensibly.

"What could have happened, however, puzzled me sorely. As I made my hurried preparations for setting out I fairly perplexed myself with speculation. I went into the kitchen, where his messenger was eating some breakfast, and asked if Mr. Crawley was ill.

" 'I dinna ken,' he answered. 'He mad' no complaint, but he luiked awful bad, just awful.'

" 'In what way?' I inquired.

" 'As if he had seen a ghaist,' was the reply.

"This made me very uneasy, and I jumped to the conclusion the trouble was connected with money matters. Young men will be young men." Here the minister looked significantly at the callow bird of our company, a youth who had never owed a sixpence in his life or given away a cent; while Jack Hill—no chicken, by the way— was over head and ears in debt, and could not keep a sovereign in his pocket, though spending or bestowing it involved going dinnerless the next day.

"Young men will be young men," repeated the minister, in his best pulpit manner ("Just as though any one expected them to be young women!" grumbled Jack to me afterwards), "and I feared that now he was settled and comfortably off, some old creditor he had been paying as best he could, might have become pressing. I knew nothing of his liabilities, or, beyond the amount of the stipend paid him, the state of his pecuniary affairs; but, having once in my own life made myself responsible for a debt, I was aware of all the trouble putting your arm out further than you can draw it back involves. And I considered that most probably money, which is the root of all evil" ("and all good" Jack's eyes suggested to me), "was the cause of my young friend's agony of mind. Blessed with a large family—every one of whom is now alive and doing well, I thank God, out in the world—you may imagine I had not much opportunity for laying by. Still, I had put aside a little for a rainy day, and that little I placed in my pocket-book, hoping even a small sum might prove of use in case of emergency.'

"By the road," proceeded our host, "Dendeldy is distant from here ten long miles, but by a short cut across the hills it can be reached in something under six. For me it was nothing of a walk, and accordingly I arrived at the manse ere noon."

He paused, and, though thirty years had elapsed, drew a handkerchief across his forehead before he continued his narrative.

"I had to climb a steep brae to reach the front door, but before I could breast it my friend met me.

" 'Thank God you are come,' he said, pressing my hand in his. 'Oh, I am grateful.'

"He was trembling with excitement. His face was a ghastly pallor. His voice was that of a person suffering from some terrible shock, labouring under some awful fear.

" 'What *has* happened, Edward?' I asked. I had known him since he was a little boy. 'I am distressed to see you in such a state. Rouse yourself; be a man; whatever may have gone wrong can possibly be righted. I have come over to do all that lies in my power for you. If it is a matter of money——'

" 'No, no; it is not money,' he interrupted; 'would that it were!' and he began to tremble again so violently that really he communicated some part of his nervousness to me, and put me into a state of perfect terror.

" 'Whatever it is, Crawley, out with it,' I said; 'have you murdered anybody?'

" 'No, it is worse than that,' he answered.

" 'But that's just nonsense,' I declared. 'Are you in your right mind, do you think?'

" 'I wish I were not,' he returned. 'I'd like to know I was stark staring mad; it would be happier for me—far, far happier.'

" 'If you don't tell me this minute what is the matter, I shall turn on my heel and tramp my way home again,' I said, half in anger at what I thought was his folly.

" 'Come into the house,' he entreated, 'and try to have patience with me; for indeed, Mr. Morison, I am sorely troubled. I have been through my deep waters, and they have gone clean over my head.'

"We went into his little study and sat down. For a while he remained silent, his head resting upon his hand, struggling with some strong emotion; but after about five minutes he asked in a low subdued voice:

" 'Do you believe in dreams?'

" 'What has my belief to do with the matter in hand?' I inquired.

" 'It is a dream, an awful dream, that is troubling me.'

"I rose from my chair.

" 'Do you mean to say,' I asked, 'you have brought me from my business and my parish to tell me you have had a bad dream?'

" 'That is just what I do mean to say,' he answered. 'At least it was not a dream—it was a vision; no, I don't mean a vision—I can't tell you what it was; but nothing I ever went through in actual life was half so real, and I have bound myself to go through it all again. There is no hope for me, Mr. Morison. I sit before you a lost creature, the most miserable man on the face of the whole earth.'

" 'What did you dream?' I inquired.

"A dreadful fit of trembling again seized him; but at last he managed to say: 'I have been like this ever since, and I shall be like this for evermore, till—till—the end comes.'

" 'When did you have your bad dream?' I asked.

" 'Last night, or rather this morning,' he answered. 'I'll tell you all about it. I was as well when I went to bed about eleven o'clock as ever I was in my life. I had been considering my sermon and felt satisfied I should be able to deliver a good one next Sunday morning. I had taken nothing after my tea and I lay down in my bed feeling at peace with all mankind, and satisfied with my lot. How long I slept, or what I dreamt about at first, if I dreamt at all, I don't know; but after a time the mists seemed to clear from before my eyes, to roll away like clouds from a mountain summit, and I found myself walking on a beautiful summer's evening beside the River Deldy.'

"He paused for a moment, and an irrepressible shudder shook his frame.

" 'Go on,' I said, for I felt afraid of his breaking down again.

"He looked at me pitifully, with a hungry entreaty in his weary eyes, and continued.

" 'It was a lovely evening and I never thought the earth had looked so beautiful before. I walked on and on, till I came to that point where, as you may perhaps remember, the path, growing very narrow, winds round the base of a great crag, and leads the wayfarer suddenly into a little green amphitheatre, bounded on one side by the river, and on the other by rocks, that rise in places sheer to a height of a hundred feet or more.'

" 'I remember it,' I said; 'a little farther on three streams meet and fall with a tremendous roar into the Witches' Cauldron. A fine sight in the winter time, only there is scarce any reaching it from below, as the path you mention and the little green oasis are mostly covered with water.'

" 'I had not been there before since I was a child,' he went on mournfully, 'but I recollected it as one of the most solitary spots possible; and my astonishment was great, to see a man standing in the pathway, with a drawn sword in his hand. He did not stir as I drew near, so I stepped aside on the grass. Instantly he barred my way.

" ' "You can't pass here," he said.

" ' "Why not?" I asked.

" ' "Because I say so," he answered.

" ' "And who are you that say so?" I inquired, looking full at him.

" 'He was like a god. Majesty and power were written on every feature, were expressed in every gesture. But, oh, the awful scorn of his smile, the contempt with which he regarded me! The beams of the setting sun fell full upon him, and seemed to bring out, as in letters of fire, the wickedness and terrible beauty of his face.

" 'I felt afraid; but I managed to say:

" ' "Stand out of my way, the river bank is as free to me as to you."

" ' "Not this part of it," he answered; "this place belongs to me."

" ' "Very well," I agreed, for I did not want to stand there bandying words with him, and a sudden darkness seemed to be falling around. "It is getting late, and so I'll turn round."

" 'He gave a laugh, the like of which never fell on human ear before, and made reply: "You can't turn back—of your own free will you have come on my ground and from it there is no return."

" 'I did not speak; I only just turned round and made as fast as I could for the path at the foot of the crag. He did not pass me, yet before I could reach the point I desired he stood barring my progress, with the scornful smile still on his lips, and his gigantic form assuming tremendous proportions in the narrow way.

" ' "Let me pass," I entreated, "and I will never come here again, never trespass more on your ground."

" ' "No, you shall not pass."

" ' "Who are you that takes such power on yourself?" I asked.

" ' "Come closer, and I will tell you," he said.

" 'I drew a step nearer, and he spoke one word. I never heard it before, but, by some extraordinary intuition, I knew what it meant. He was the Evil One. The name seemed to be taken up by the echoes, and repeated from rock to rock and crag to crag. The whole air seemed full of that one word—and then a great horror of darkness came about us, only the place where we stood remained light. We occupied a small circle walled round with the thick blackness of night.

" ' "You must come with me," he said.

" 'I refused and then he threatened me. I implored and entreated and wept, but at last I agreed to do what he wanted if he would promise to let me return. Again he laughed, and said, Yes, I should return—and the rocks and trees and mountains, ay, and the very rivers, seemed to take up the answer and bear it in sobbing whispers away into the darkness.'

"He stopped, and lay back in his chair, shivering like one in an ague fit.

" 'Go on,' I repeated again, 'it was only a dream, you know.'

" 'Was it?' he murmured, mournfully. 'Ah, you have not heard the end of it yet.'

" 'Let me hear it then,' I said. 'What happened afterwards?'

" 'The darkness seemed in part to clear away and we walked side by side across the grass in the twilight, straight up to the bare, black wall of rock. With the hilt of his sword he struck a heavy blow, and the solid rock opened as though it were a door. We passed through and it closed behind us with a tremendous clang—yes, it closed behind us'; and at that point he fairly broke down, crying and sobbing as I had never seen a man even in the most frightful grief cry and sob before."

The minister paused in his narrative. At that moment there came a tremendous blast of wind which shook the windows of the manse, and burst open the hall door, and caused the candles to flicker and the fire to go roaring up the chimney. It is not too much to say that, what with the uncanny story, and the howling storm, we all felt that creeping sort of uneasiness which so often seems like the touch of something from another world—a hand stretched across the bound-ary-line of time and eternity, the coldness and mystery of which make the stoutest heart tremble.

"I am telling you this tale," said Mr. Morison, resuming his seat after a brief absence to see that the fastenings of the house were properly attended to, "exactly as I heard it. You must draw your own deductions from the facts I put before you. Part of that great and terrible region in which he found himself, my friend went on to tell me, he penetrated, compelled by a power he could not resist, to see the most awful sights and the most frightful sufferings. There was no form of vice that had not there its representative. As they moved along, his companion told him the special sin for which such horrible punishment was being inflicted. Shuddering, and in mortal agony, he was unable to withdraw his eyes from the dreadful spectacle. The atmosphere grew more unendurable, the sights more and more terrible, the cries, groans, blasphemies more awful and heart-rending.

" 'I can bear no more,' he gasped at last; 'let me go!'

"With a mocking laugh, the Presence beside him answered the appeal; a laugh which was taken up, even by the lost and anguished spirits around.

" 'There is no return' said the pitiless voice.

" 'But you promised,' he cried, 'you promised me faithfully.'

" 'What are promises here?' and the words were the sound of doom.

"Still he prayed and entreated; he fell on his knees and in his agony spoke words that seemed to cause the purpose of the Evil One to falter.

" 'You shall go,' he said, 'on one condition: that you agree to return to me on Wednesday next—or send a substitute.'

" 'I could not do that,' said my friend. 'I could not send any fellow-creature here. Better stop myself than do that.'

" 'Then stop,' said Satan, with the bitterest contempt; and he was turning away when the poor distracted soul asked for a minute more before he made his choice.

"He was in an awful strait: on the one hand, how could he remain himself? on the other, how could he doom another to such fearful torments? Who could he send? Who would come? And then suddenly there flashed into his mind the thought of an old man to whom it could not signify much whether he took up his place in this abode a few days sooner or a few days later. He was travelling to it as fast as he knew how. He was the reprobate of the parish; the sinner without hope that successive ministers had striven in vain to reclaim from the error of his ways; a man marked and doomed—Sandy the Tinker. Sandy, who was mostly drunk and always godless. Sandy, who, it was said, believed in nothing, and gloried in his infidelity. Sandy, whose soul really did not signify much. He would send him. Lifting his eyes, he saw those of his tormentor surveying him scornfully.

" 'Well, have you made your choice?' he asked.

" 'Yes, I think I can send a substitute,' was the hesitating answer.

" 'See you do then,' was the reply; 'for if you do not, and fail to return yourself, *I shall come for you.* Wednesday, remember, before midnight.' And with these words ringing in his ears he was flung violently through the rock, and found himself in the middle of his bedroom floor, as if he had just been kicked there.

"This is not the end of the story, is it?" asked one of our party, as the minister came to a full stop, and looked earnestly at the fire.

"No," he answered, "it is not the end; but before proceeding I must ask you to bear carefully in mind the circumstances already recounted. Especially remember the date mentioned—*Wednesday next, before midnight.*

" Whatever I thought, and you may think, about my friend's dream, it made the most remarkable impression upon *his* mind. He could not shake off its influence; he passed from one state of nervousness to another. It was in vain I entreated him to exert his common sense, and call all his strength of mind to his assistance. I might as well have spoken to the wind. He implored me not to leave him, and I agreed to remain. Indeed, to leave him in his then frame of mind would have been an act of the greatest cruelty. He wanted me also to preach in his place on the Sunday following; but this I flatly refused.

" 'If you do not make an effort now,' I said, 'you will never make it. Rouse yourself, get on with your sermon, and if you buckle down to work you will soon forget all about that foolish dream.'

" Well, to cut a long story short, the sermon was somehow composed and Sunday came, and my friend, a little better and getting over his fret, walked up into the pulpit to preach. He looked dreadfully ill; but I thought the worst was over now and that he would go on mending.

"Vain hope! He gave out the text and then looked over the congregation—and the first person on whom his eyes lighted was Sandy the Tinker. Sandy, who had never before been known to enter a place of worship of any sort; Sandy, whom he had mentally chosen as his substitute, and who was *due on the following Wednesday* —sitting just below him, quite sober, and comparatively clean, waiting with a great show of attention for the opening words of the sermon.

"With a terrible cry my friend caught the front of the pulpit, then swayed back and fell down in a fainting fit. He was carried home and a doctor sent for. I said a few words, addressed apparently to the congregation, but really to Sandy, for my heart somehow came into my mouth at the sight of him. And then, after I had dismissed the people, I paced slowly back to the manse, almost afraid of what might meet me.

"Mr. Crawley was not dead; but he was in the most dreadful state of physical exhaustion and mental agitation. It was dreadful to hear him. How could he go himself? How could he send Sandy?—poor old Sandy whose soul, in the sight of God, was just as precious as his own.

"His whole cry was for us to deliver him from the Evil One; to save him from committing a sin which would render him a wretched man for life. He counted the hours and the minutes before he must return to that horrible place.

" 'I can't send Sandy,' he would moan. 'I cannot. Oh, I cannot save myself at such a price!'

"And then he would cover his face with the bedclothes, only to start up and wildly entreat me not to leave him; to stand between the enemy and himself, to save him, or, if that were impossible, to give him the courage to do what was right.

" 'If this continues,' said the doctor, 'Wednesday will find him either dead or a raving lunatic.'

"We talked the matter over, the doctor and I, as we walked to and fro in the meadow behind the manse; and we decided, having to make our choice of two evils, to risk giving him such an opiate as should carry him over the dreaded interval. We knew it was a perilous thing to do even with one in his condition, but, as I said before, we could only take the lesser of two evils.

"What we dreaded most was his awaking before the time expired, so I kept watch beside him. He lay like one dead through the whole of Tuesday night and Wednesday and Wednesday evening. Eight, nine, ten, eleven o'clock came and passed—then twelve. 'God be thanked!' I said, as I stooped over him and heard he was breathing quietly.

" 'He will do now, I hope,' said the doctor, who had come in just before midnight, 'You will stay with him till he wakes?'

"I promised that I would and in the beautiful dawn of a summer's morning he opened his eyes and smiled. He had no recollection then of what had occurred; he was as weak as an infant and when I bade him try to go to sleep again turned on his pillow and sank to rest once more.

"Worn out with watching, I stepped softly from the room and passed into the fresh, sweet air. I strolled down to the garden-gate, and stood looking at the great mountains and the fair country, and the Deldy wandering like a silver thread through the green fields below.

"All at once my attention was attracted by a group of people coming slowly along the road leading from the hills. I could not at first see that in their midst something was being borne on men's shoulders; but when at last I made this out, I hurried to meet them and learn what was the matter.

" 'Has there been an accident?' I asked, as I drew near.

"They stopped and one man came towards me.

" 'Ay,' he said, 'the warst accident that could befa' him, puir fella. He's deid.'

" 'Who is it?' I asked, pressing forward; and lifting the cloth they had flung over his face, I saw *Sandy the Tinker!*

" 'He had been coming home, I tak' it,' remarked one who stood by, 'puir Sandy, and gaed over the cliff afore he could save himself. We found him just on this side of the Witches's Caldron, where there's a bonny strip of green turf, and his cuddy was feeding on the hill-top with the bit cart behind her.' "

There was silence for a minute—then one of the ladies said softly, "Poor Sandy."

"And what became of Mr. Crawley?" asked the other.

"He gave up his parish and went abroad as a missionary. He is still living."

"What a most extraordinary story!" I remarked.

"Yes, I think so," said the minister. "If you like to go round by Deldy tomorrow, my son, who now occupies the manse, would show you the scene of the occurrence."

The next day we all stood looking at the frowning cliff and at the Deldy, swollen by recent rains, rushing on its way.

The youngest of the party went up to the rock and knocked upon it loudly with his cane.

"Oh, don't do that, pray!" cried both the ladies nervously—the spirit of the weird story still brooded over us.

"What do you think of the coincidence, Jack?" I inquired of my friend, as we talked apart from the others.

"Ask me when we get back to Fleet Street," he answered.

The Old House in Vauxhall Walk

I

"Houseless – homeless – hopeless!"

Many a one who had before him trodden that same street must

have uttered the same words – the weary, the desolate, the hungry, the forsaken, the waifs and strays of struggling humanity that are always coming and going, cold, starving and miserable, over the pavements of Lambeth Parish; but it is open to question whether they were ever previously spoken with a more thorough conviction of their truth, or with a feeling of keener self-pity, than by the young man who hurried along Vauxhall Walk one rainy winter's night, with no overcoat on his shoulders and no hat on his head.

A strange sentence for one-and-twenty to give expression to – and it was stranger still to come from the lips of a person who looked like and who was a gentleman. He did not appear either to have sunk very far down in the good graces of Fortune. There was no sign or token which would have induced a passer-by to imagine he had been worsted after a long fight with calamity. His boots were not worn down at the heels or broken at the toes, as many, many boots were which dragged and shuffled and scraped along the pavement. His clothes were good and fashionably cut, and innocent of the rents and patches and tatters that slunk wretchedly by, crouched in doorways, and held out a hand mutely appealing for charity. His face was not pinched with famine or lined with wicked wrinkles, or brutalised by drink and debauchery, and yet he said and thought he was hopeless, and almost in his young despair spoke the words aloud.

It was a bad night to be about with such a feeling in one's heart. The rain was cold, pitiless and increasing. A damp, keen wind blew down the cross streets leading from the river. The fumes of the gas works seemed to fall with the rain. The roadway was muddy; the pavement greasy; the lamps burned dimly; and that dreary district of London looked its very gloomiest and worst.

Certainly not an evening to be abroad without a home to go to, or a sixpence in one's pocket, yet this was the position of the young gentleman who, without a hat, strode along Vauxhall Walk, the rain beating on his unprotected head.

Upon the houses, so large and good – once inhabited by well-to-do citizens, now let out for the most part in floors to weekly tenants – he looked enviously. He would have given much to have had a room, or even part of one. He had been walking for a long time, ever since dark in fact, and dark falls soon in December. He was tired and cold and hungry, and he saw no prospect save of pacing the streets all night.

As he passed one of the lamps, the light falling on his face revealed handsome young features, a mobile, sensitive mouth, and that particular formation of the eyebrows – not a frown exactly, but a certain draw of the brows – often considered to bespeak genius, but which more surely accompanies an impulsive organisation easily pleased, easily depressed, capable of suffering very keenly or of enjoying fully. In his short life he had not enjoyed much, and he had suffered a good deal. That night when he walked bareheaded through the rain, affairs had come to a crisis. So far as he in his despair felt able to see or reason, the best thing he could do was to die. The world did not want him; he would be better out of it.

The door of one of the houses stood open, and he could see in the dimly lighted hall some few articles of furniture waiting to be removed. A van stood beside the curb, and two men were lifting a table into it as he, for a second, paused.

"Ah," he thought, "even those poor people have some place to go to, some shelter provided, while I have not a roof to cover my head, or a shilling to get a night's lodging." And he went on fast, as if memory were spurring him, so fast that a man running after had some trouble to overtake him.

"Master Graham! Master Graham!" this man exclaimed, breathlessly; and, thus addressed, the young fellow stopped as if he had been shot.

"Who are you that know me?" he asked, facing round.

"I'm William; don't you remember William, Master Graham? And, Lord's sake, sir, what are you doing out a night like this without your hat?"

"I forgot it," was the answer, "and I did not care to go back and fetch it."

"Then why don't you buy another, sir? You'll catch your death of cold; and besides, you'll excuse me, sir, but it does look odd."

"I know that," said Master Graham grimly, "but I haven't a halfpenny in the world."

"Have you and the Master, then –" began the man, but there e hesitated and stopped.

"Had a quarrel? Yes, and one that will last us our lives," finished the other, with a bitter laugh.

"And where are you going now?"

"Going! Nowhere, except to seek out the softest paving stone, or the shelter of an arch."

"You are joking, sir."

"I don't feel much in a mood for jesting either."

"Will you come back with me, Master Graham? We are just at the last of our moving, but there is a spark of fire still in the grate, and it would be better talking out of this rain. Will you come, sir?"

"Come! Of course I will come," said the young fellow, and, turning, they retraced their steps to the house he had looked into as he passed along.

An old, old house, with long, wide hall, stairs low, easy of ascent, with deep cornices to the ceilings, and oak floorings, and mahogany doors, which still spoke mutely of the wealth and stability of the original owner, who lived before the Tradescants and Ashmoles were thought of, and had been sleeping for longer than they, in St. Mary's churchyard, hard by the archbishop's palace.

"Step upstairs, sir," entreated the departing tenant; "it's cold down here, with the door standing wide."

"Had you the whole house, then, William?" asked Graham Coulton, in some surprise.

"The whole of it, and right sorry I, for one, am to leave it; but nothing else would serve my wife. This room, sir," and with a little conscious pride, William, doing the honours of his late residence, asked his guest into a spacious apartment occupying the full width of the house on the first floor.

Tired though he was, the young man could not repress an exclamation of astonishment.

"Why, we have nothing so large as this at home, William," he said.

"It's a fine house," answered William, raking the embers

together as he spoke and throwing some wood upon them; "but, like many a good family, it has come down in the world."

There were four windows in the room, shuttered close; they had deep, low seats, suggestive of pleasant days gone by; when, well-curtained and well-cushioned, they formed snug retreats for the children, and sometimes for adults also; there was no furniture left, unless an oaken settle beside the hearth, and a large mirror let into the panelling at the opposite end of the apartment, with a black marble console table beneath it, could be so considered; but the very absence of chairs and tables enabled the magnificent proportions of the chamber to be seen to full advantage, and there was nothing to distract the attention from the ornamented ceiling, the panelled walls, the old-world chimney-piece so quaintly carved, and the fire-place lined with tiles, each one of which contained a picture of some scriptural or allegorical subject.

"Had you been staying on here, William," said Coulton, flinging himself wearily on the settee, "I'd have asked you to let me stop where I am for the night."

"If you can make shift, sir, there is nothing as I am aware of to prevent you stopping," answered the man, fanning the wood into a flame. "I shan't take the key back to the landlord till to-morrow, and this would be better for you than the cold streets at any rate."

"Do you really mean what you say?" asked the other eagerly. "I should be thankful to lie here; I feel dead beat."

"Then stay, Master Graham, and welcome. I'll fetch a basket of coals I was going to put in the van, and make up a good fire, so that you can warm yourself; then I must run round to the other house for a minute or two, but it's not far, and I'll be back as soon as ever I can."

"Thank you, William; you were always good to me," said the young man gratefully. "This is delightful," and he stretched his numbed hands over the blazing wood, and looked round the room with a satisfied smile.

"I did not expect to get into such quarters," he remarked, as his friend in need reappeared, carrying a half-bushel basket full of coals, with which he proceeded to make up a roaring fire. "I am sure the last thing I could have imagined was meeting with anyone I knew in Vauxhall Walk."

"Where were you coming from, Master Graham?" asked William curiously.

"From old Melfield's. I was at his school once, you know, and he has now retired, and is living upon the proceeds of years of robbery in Kennington Oval. I thought, perhaps he would lend me a pound, or offer me a night's lodging, or even a glass of wine; but, oh dear, no. He took the moral tone, and observed he could have nothing to say to a son who defied his father's authority. He gave me plenty of advice, but nothing else, and showed me out into the rain with a bland courtesy, for which I could have struck him."

William muttered something under his breath which was not a blessing, and added aloud:

"You are better here, sir, I think, at any rate. I'll be back in less than half an hour."

Left to himself, young Coulton took off his coat, and shifting the settle a little, hung it over the end to dry. With his hand-kerchief he rubbed some of the wet out of his hair; then, perfectly exhausted, he lay down before the fire and, pillowing his head on his arm, fell fast asleep.

He was awakened nearly an hour afterwards by the sound of someone gently stirring the fire and moving quietly about the room. Starting into a sitting posture, he looked around him, bewildered for a moment, and then, recognising his humble friend, said laughingly:

"I had lost myself; I could not imagine where I was."

"I am sorry to see you here, sir," was the reply; "but still this is better than being out of doors. It has come on a nasty night. I brought a rug round with me that, perhaps, you would wrap yourself in."

"I wish, at the same time, you had brought me something to eat," said the young man, laughing.

"Are you hungry, then, sir?" asked William, in a tone of concern.

"Yes; I have had nothing to eat since breakfast. The governor and I commenced rowing the minute we sat down to luncheon, and I rose and left the table. But hunger does not signify; I am dry and warm, and can forget the other matter in sleep."

"And it's too late now to buy anything," soliloquised the man; "the shops are all shut long ago. Do you think, sir," he added, brightening, "you could manage some bread and cheese?"

"Do I think – I should call it a perfect feast," answered Graham Coulton. "But never mind about food to-night, William; you have had trouble enough, and to spare, already."

William's only answer was to dart to the door and run downstairs. Presently he reappeared, carrying in one hand bread and cheese wrapped up in paper, and in the other a pewter measure full of beer.

"It's the best I could do, sir," he said apologetically. "I had to beg this from the landlady."

"Here's to her good health!" exclaimed the young fellow gaily, taking a long pull at the tankard. "That tastes better than champagne in my father's house."

"Won't he be uneasy about you?" ventured William, who, having by this time emptied the coals, was now seated on the inverted basket, looking wistfully at the relish with which the son of the former master was eating his bread and cheese.

"No," was the decided answer. "When he hears it pouring cats and dogs he will only hope I am out in the deluge, and say a good drenching will cool my pride."

"I do not think you are right there," remarked the man.

"But I am sure I am. My father always hated me, as he hated my mother."

"Begging your pardon, sir; he was over fond of your mother."

"If you had heard what he said about her to-day, you might find reason to alter your opinion. He told me I resembled her in mind as well as body; that I was a coward, a simpleton, and a hypocrite."

"He did not mean it, sir."

"He did, every word. He does think I am a coward, because I– I –" and the young fellow broke into a passion of hysterical tears.

"I don't half like leaving you here alone," said William,

glancing round the room with a quick trouble in his eyes; "but I have no place fit to ask you to stop, and I am forced to go myself, because I am night watchman, and must be on at twelve o'clock."

"I shall be right enough," was the answer. "Only I mustn't talk any more of my father. Tell me about yourself, William. How did you manage to get such a big house, and why are you leaving it?"

"The landlord put me in charge, sir; and it was my wife's fancy not to like it.".

"Why did she not like it?"

"She felt desolate alone with the children at night," answered William, turning away his head; then added, next minute; "Now, sir, if you think I can do no more for you, I had best be off. Time's getting on. I'll look round to-morrow morning."

"Good night," said the young fellow, stretching out his hand, which the other took as freely and frankly as it was offered. "What should I have done this evening if I had not chanced to meet you?"

"I don't think there is much chance in the world, Master Graham," was the quiet answer. "I do hope you will rest well, and not be the worse for your wetting."

"No fear of that," was the rejoinder, and the next minute the young man found himself all alone in the Old House in Vauxhall Walk.

II

Lying on the settle, with the fire burnt out, and the room in total darkness, Graham Coulton dreamed a curious dream. He thought he awoke from deep slumber to find a log smouldering away upon the hearth, and the mirror at the end of the apartment reflecting fitful gleams of light. He could not understand how it came to pass that, far away as he was from the glass, he was able to see everything in it; but he resigned himself to the difficulty without astonishment, as people generally do in dreams.

Neither did he feel surprised when he beheld the outline of a female figure seated beside the fire, engaged in picking something out of her lap and dropping it with a despairing gesture.

He heard the mellow sound of gold, and knew she was lifting and dropping sovereigns. He turned a little so as to see the person engaged in such a singular and meaningless manner, and found that, where there had been no chair on the previous night, there was a chair now, on which was seated an old, wrinkled hag, her clothes poor and ragged, a mob cap barely covering her scant white hair, her cheeks sunken, her nose hooked, her fingers more like talons than aught else as they dived down into the heap of gold, portions of which they lifted but to scatter mournfully.

"Oh! my lost life," she moaned, in a voice of the bitterest anguish. "Oh! my lost life – for one day, for one hour of it again!"

Out of the darkness – out of the corner of the room where the shadows lay deepest – out from the gloom abiding near the door – out from the dreary night, with their sodden feet and the wet dripping from their heads, came the old men and the young children, the worn women and the weary hearts, whose misery that gold might have relieved, but whose wretchedness it mocked.

Round that miser, who once sat gloating as she now sat lamenting, they crowded – all those pale, sad shapes – the aged of days, the infant of hours, the sobbing outcast, honest poverty, repentant vice; but one low cry proceeded from those pale lips – a cry for help she might have given, but which she withheld.

They closed about her, all together, as they had done singly in life; they prayed, they sobbed, they entreated; with haggard eyes the figure regarded the poor she had repulsed, the children against whose cry she had closed her ears, the old people she had suffered to starve and die for want of what would have been the merest trifle to her; then, with a terrible scream, she raised her lean arms above her head, and sank down – down – the gold scattering as it fell out of her lap, and rolling along the floor, till its gleam was lost in the outer darkness beyond.

Then Graham Coulton awoke in good earnest, with the perspiration oozing from every pore, with a fear and an agony upon him such as he had never before felt in all his existence, and with the sound of the heart-rending cry – "Oh! my lost life" – still ringing in his ears.

Mingled with all, too, there seemed to have been some lesson for him which he had forgotten, that, try as he would, eluded his memory, and which, in the very act of waking, glided away.

He lay for a little thinking about all this, and then, still heavy with sleep, retraced his way into dreamland once more.

It was natural, perhaps, that, mingling with the strange fantasies which follow in the train of night and darkness, the former vision should recur, and the young man ere long found himself toiling through scene after scene wherein the figure of the woman he had seen seated beside a dying fire held principal place.

He saw her walking slowly across the floor munching a dry crust – she who could have purchased all the luxuries wealth can command; on the hearth, contemplating her, stood a man of commanding presence, dressed in the fashion of long ago. In his eyes there was a dark look of anger, on his lips a curling smile of disgust, and somehow, even in his sleep, the dreamer understood it was the ancestor to the descendant he beheld – that the house put to mean uses in which he lay had never so far descended from its high estate, as the woman possessed of so pitiful a soul, contaminated with the most despicable and insidious vice poor humanity knows, for all other vices seem to have connection with the flesh, but the greed of the miser eats into the very soul.

Filthy of person, repulsive to look at, hard of heart as she was, he yet beheld another phantom, which, coming into the room, met her almost on the threshold, taking her by the hand, and pleading, as it seemed, for assistance. He could not hear all that passed, but a word now and then fell upon his car. Some talk of former days; some mention of a fair young mother – an appeal, as it seemed, to a time when they were tiny brother and sister, and the accursed greed for gold had not divided them. All in vain; the hag only answered him as she had answered the children, and the young girls, and the old people in his former vision. Her heart was as invulnerable to natural affection as it had proved to human sympathy. He begged, as it appeared, for aid to avert some bitter misfortune or terrible disgrace, and adamant might have been found more yielding to his prayer. Then the figure standing on the hearth changed to an angel, which folded its wings mournfully over its face, and the man, with bowed head, slowly left the room.

Even as he did so the scene changed again; it was night once more, and the miser wended her way upstairs. From below, Graham Coulton fancied he watched her toiling wearily from step to step. She had aged strangely since the previous scenes. She moved with difficulty; it seemed the greatest exertion for her to creep from step to step, her skinny hand traversing the balusters with slow and painful deliberateness. Fascinated, the young man's eyes followed the progress of that feeble, decrepit woman. She was solitary in a desolate house, with a deeper blackness than the darkness of night waiting to engulf her.

It seemed to Graham Coulton that after that he lay for a time in a still, dreamless sleep, upon awakening from which he found himself entering a chamber as sordid and unclean in its appointments as the woman of his previous vision had been in her person. The poorest labourer's wife would have gathered more comforts around her than that room contained. A four-poster bedstead without hangings of any kind – a blind drawn up awry – an old carpet covered with dust, and dirt on the floor – a rickety washstand with all the paint worn off it – an ancient mahogany dressing table, and a cracked glass spotted all over – were all the objects he could at first discern, looking at the room through that dim light which oftentimes obtains in dreams.

By degrees, however, he perceived the outline of someone lying huddled on the bed. Drawing nearer, he found it was that of the person whose dreadful presence seemed to pervade the house. What a terrible sight she looked, with her thin white locks scattered over the pillow, with what were mere remnants of blankets gathered about her shoulders, with her claw-like fingers clutching the clothes, as though even in sleep she was guarding her gold!

An awful and a repulsive spectacle, but not with half the terror in it of that which followed. Even as the young man looked he heard stealthy footsteps on the stairs. Then he saw first one man and then his fellow steal cautiously into the room. Another second, and the pair stood beside the bed, murder in their eyes.

Graham Coulton tried to shout – tried to move, but the

deterrent power which exists in dreams only tied his tongue and paralysed his limbs. He could but hear and look, and what he heard and saw was this: aroused suddenly from sleep, the woman started, only to receive a blow from one of the ruffians, whose fellow followed his lead by plunging a knife into her breast.

Then, with a gurgling scream, she fell back on the bed, and at the same moment, with a cry, Graham Coulton again awoke, to thank heaven it was but an illusion.

III

"I hope you slept well, sir." It was William, who, coming into the hall with the sunlight of a fine bright morning streaming after him, asked this question: "Had you a good night's rest?"

Graham Coulton laughed, and answered:

"Why, faith, I was somewhat in the case of Paddy, 'who could not slape for dhraming'. I slept well enough, I suppose, but whether it was in consequence of the row with my dad, or the hard bed, or the cheese – most likely the bread and cheese so late at night – I dreamt all the night long, the most extraordinary dreams. Some old woman kept cropping up, and I saw her murdered."

"You don't say that, sir?" said William nervously.

"I do, indeed," was the reply. "However, that is all gone and past. I have been down in the kitchen and had a good wash, and I am as fresh as a daisy, and as hungry as a hunter; and, oh, William, can you get me any breakfast?"

"Certainly, Master Graham, I have brought round a kettle, and I will make the water boil immediately. I suppose, sir" – this tentatively – "you'll be going home to-day?"

"Home!" repeated the young man. "Decidedly not. I'll never go home again till I return with some medal hung to my coat, or a leg or arm cut off. I've thought it all out, William. I'll go and enlist. There's a talk of war; and, living or dead, my father shall have reason to retract his opinion about my being a coward."

"I am sure the admiral never thought you anything of the sort, sir," said William. "Why, you have the pluck of ten!"

"Not before him," answered the young fellow sadly.

"You'll do nothing rash, Master Graham; you won't go 'listing, or aught of that sort, in your anger?"

"If I do not, what is to become of me?" asked the other. "I cannot dig – to beg I am ashamed. Why, but for you, I should not have had a roof over my head last night."

"Not much of a roof, I am afraid, sir."

"Not much of a roof!" repeated the young man. "Why, who could desire a better? What a capital room this is," he went on, looking around the apartment, where William was now kindling a fire; "one might dine twenty people here easily!"

"If you think so well of the place, Master Graham, you might stay here for a while, till you have made up your mind what you are going to do. The landlord won't make any objection, I am very sure."

"Oh! nonsense; he would want a long rent for a house like this."

"I daresay; *if he could get it*," was William's significant answer.

"What do you mean? Won't the place let?"

"No, sir. I did not tell you last night, but there was a murder done here, and people are shy of the house ever since."

"A murder! What sort of a murder? Who was murdered?"

"A woman, Master Graham – the landlord's sister; she lived here all alone, and was supposed to have money. Whether she had or not, she was found dead from a stab in her breast, and if there ever was any money, it must have been taken at the same time, for none ever was found in the house from that day to this."

"Was that the reason your wife would not stop here?" asked the young man, leaning against the mantelshelf, and looking thoughtfully down on William.

"Yes, sir. She could not stand it any longer; she got that thin and nervous no one would have believed it possible; she never saw anything, but she said she heard footsteps and voices, and then when she walked through the hall, or up the staircase, someone always seemed to be following her. We put the children to sleep in that big room you had last night, and they declared they often saw an old woman sitting by the hearth. Nothing ever came my way," finished William, with a laugh; "I

48

was always ready to go to sleep the minute my head touched the pillow."

"Were not the murderers discovered?" asked Graham Coulton.

"No, sir; the landlord, Miss Tynan's brother, had always lain under the suspicion of it – quite wrongfully, I am very sure – but he will never clear himself now. It was known he came and asked her for help a day or two before the murder, and it was also known he was able within a week or two to weather whatever trouble had been harassing him. Then, you see, the money was never found; and, altogether, people scarce knew what to think."

"Humph!" ejaculated Graham Coulton, and he took a few turns up and down the apartment. "Could I go and see this landlord?"

"Surely, sir, if you had a hat," answered William, with such a serious decorum that the young man burst out laughing.

"That is an obstacle, certainly," he remarked, "and I must make a note do instead. I have a pencil in my pocket, so here goes."

Within half an hour from the dispatch of that note William was back again with a sovereign; the landlord's compliments, and he would be much obliged if Mr. Coulton could "step round."

"You'll do nothing rash, sir," entreated William.

"Why, man," answered the young fellow, "one may as well be picked off by a ghost as a bullet. What is there to be afraid of?"

William only shook his head. He did not think his young master was made of the stuff likely to remain alone in a haunted house and solve the mystery it assuredly contained by dint of his own unassisted endeavours. And yet when Graham Coulton came out of the landlord's house he looked more bright and gay than usual, and walked up the Lambeth road to the place where Wiliam awaited his return, humming an air as he paced along.

"We have settled the matter," he said. "And now if the dad wants his son for Christmas, it will trouble him to find him."

"Don't say that, Master Graham, don't," entreated the man, with a shiver; "maybe after all it would have been better if you had never happened to chance upon Vauxhall Walk."

"Don't croak, William," answered the young man; "if it was not the best day's work I ever did for myself I'm a Dutchman."

During the whole of that afternoon, Graham Coulton searched diligently for the missing treasure Mr. Tynan assured him had never been discovered. Youth is confident, and self-opinionated, and this fresh explorer felt satisfied that, though others had failed, he would be successful. On the second floor he found one door locked, but he did not pay much attention to that at the moment, as he believed if there was anything concealed it was more likely to be found in the lower than the upper part of the house. Late into the evening he pursued his researches in the kitchen and cellars and old-fashioned cupboards, of which the basement had an abundance.

It was nearly eleven, when, engaged in poking about amongst the empty bins of a wine cellar as large as a family vault, he suddenly felt a rush of cold air at his back. Moving, his candle was instantly extinguished, and in the very moment of being left in darkness he saw, standing in the doorway, a woman, resembling her who had haunted his dreams overnight.

He rushed with outstretched hands to seize her, but clutched only air. He relit his candle, and closely examined the basement, shutting off communication with the ground floor ere doing so. All in vain. Not a trace could he find of living creature – not a window was open – not a door unbolted.

"It is very odd," he thought, as, after securely fastening the door at the top of the staircase, he searched the whole upper portion of the house, with the exception of the one room mentioned.

"I must get the key of that to-morrow," he decided, standing gloomily with his back to the fire and his eyes wandering about the drawing-room, where he had once again taken up his abode.

Even as the thought passed through his mind, he saw standing in the open doorway a woman with white dishevelled hair, clad in mean garments, ragged and dirty. She lifted her hand and shook it at him with a menacing gesture, and then, just as he was darting towards her, a wonderful thing occurred.

From behind the great mirror there glided a second female

figure, at the sight of which the first turned and fled, uttering piercing shrieks as the other followed her from storey to storey.

Sick almost with terror, Graham Coulton watched the dreadful pair as they fled upstairs past the locked room to the top of the house.

It was a few minutes before he recovered his self-possession. When he did so, and searched the upper apartments, he found them totally empty.

That night, ere lying down before the fire, he carefully locked and bolted the drawing-room door; before he did more he drew the heavy settle in front of it, so that if the lock were forced no entrance could be effected without considerable noise.

For some time he lay awake, then dropped into a deep sleep, from which he was awakened suddenly by a noise as if of something scuffling stealthily behind the wainscot. He raised himself on his elbow and listened, and, to his consternation, beheld seated at the opposite side of the hearth the same woman he had seen before in his dreams, lamenting over her gold.

The fire was not quite out, and at the moment shot up a last tongue of flame. By the light, transient as it was, he saw that the figure pressed a ghostly finger to its lips, and by the turn of his head and the attitude of its body seemed to be listening.

He listened also – indeed, he was too much frightened to do aught else; more and more distinct grew the sounds which had aroused him, a stealthy rustling coming nearer and nearer – up and up it seemed, behind the wainscot.

"It is rats," thought the young man, though, indeed, his teeth were almost chattering in his head with fear. But then in a moment he saw what disabused him of that idea – *the gleam of a candle or lamp through a crack in the panelling*. He tried to rise, he strove to shout – all in vain; and, sinking down, remembered nothing more till he awoke to find the grey light of an early morning stealing through one of the shutters he had left partially unclosed.

For hours after his breakfast, which he scarcely touched, long after William had left him at mid-day, Graham Coulton, having in the morning made a long and close survey of the house, sat thinking before the fire, then, apparently having made up his mind, he put on the hat he had bought, and went out.

When he returned the evening shadows were darkening down, but the pavements were full of people going marketing, for it was Christmas Eve, and all who had money to spend seemed bent on shopping.

It was terribly dreary inside the old house that night. Through the deserted rooms Graham could feel that ghostly semblance was wandering mournfully. When he turned his back he knew she was flitting from the mirror to the fire, from the fire to the mirror; but he was not afraid of her now – he was far more afraid of another matter he had taken in hand that day.

The horror of the silent house grew and grew upon him. He could hear the beating of his own heart in the dead quietude which reigned from garret to cellar.

At last William came; but the young man said nothing to him of what was in his mind. He talked to him cheerfully and hopefully enough – wondered where his father would think he had got to, and hoped Mr. Tynan might send him some Christmas pudding. Then the man said it was time for him to go, and, when Mr. Coulton went downstairs to the hall-door, remarked the key was not in it.

"No," was the answer, "I took it out to-day, to oil it."

"It wanted oiling," agreed William, "for it worked terribly stiff." Having uttered which truism he departed.

Very slowly the young man retraced his way to the drawing-room, where he only paused to lock the door on the outside; then taking off his boots he went up to the top of the house, where, entering the front attic, he waited patiently in darkness and in silence.

It was a long time, or at least it seemed long to him, before he heard the same sound which had aroused him on the previous night – a stealthy rustling – then a rush of cold air – then cautious footsteps – then the quiet opening of a door below.

It did not take as long in action as it has required to tell. In a moment the young man was out on the landing and had closed a portion of the panelling on the wall which stood open; noiselessly he crept back to the attic window, unlatched it, and sprung a rattle, the sound of which echoed far and near through the deserted streets, then rushing down the stairs, he encountered a man who, darting past him, made for the landing above; but perceiving that way of escape closed, fled down again, to find Graham struggling desperately with his fellow.

"Give him the knife – come along," he said savagely; and next instant Graham felt something like a hot iron through his shoulder, and then heard a thud, as one of the men, tripping in his rapid flight, fell from the top of the stairs to the bottom.

At the same moment there came a crash, as if the house was falling, and faint, sick, and bleeding, young Coulton lay insensible on the threshold of the room where Miss Tynan had been murdered.

When he recovered he was in the dining-room, and a doctor was examining his wound.

Near the door a policeman stiffly kept guard. The hall was full of people; all the misery and vagabondism the streets contain at that hour was crowding in to see what had happened.

Through the midst two men were being conveyed to the station-house; one, with his head dreadfully injured, on a stretcher, the other handcuffed, uttering frightful imprecations as he went.

After a time the house was cleared of the rabble, the police took possession of it, and Mr. Tynan was sent for.

"What was that dreadful noise?" asked Graham feebly, now seated on the floor, with his back resting against the wall.

'I do not know. Was there a noise?" said Mr. Tynan, humouring his fancy, as he thought.

"Yes, in the drawing-room, I think; the key is in my pocket."

Still humouring the wounded lad, Mr. Tynan took the key and ran upstairs.

When he unlocked the door, what a sight met his eyes! The mirror had fallen – it was lying all over the floor shivered into a thousand pieces; the console table had been borne down by its weight, and the marble slab was shattered as well. But this was not what chained his attention. Hundreds, thousands of gold pieces were scattered about, and an aperture behind the glass contained boxes filled with securities and deeds and bonds, the possession of which had cost his sister her life.

"Well, Graham, and what do you want?" asked Admiral Coulton that evening as his eldest born appeared before him, looking somewhat pale but otherwise unchanged.

"I want nothing," was the answer, 'but to ask your forgiveness. William has told me all the story I never knew before; and, if you let me, I will try to make it up to you for the trouble you have had. I am provided for," went on the young fellow, with a nervous laugh; 'I have made my fortune since I left you, and another man's fortune as well."

"I think you are out of your senses," said the Admiral shortly.

"No, sir, I have found them," was the answer; "and I mean to strive and make a better thing of my life than I should ever have done had I not gone to the Old House in Vauxhall Walk."

"Vauxhall Walk! What is the lad talking about?"

'I will tell you, sir, if I may sit down," was Graham Coulton's answer, and then he told this story.

THE BANSHEE'S WARNING

Many a year, before chloroform was thought of, there lived in an old rambling house, in Gerrard Street, Soho, a clever Irishman called Hertford O'Donnell.

After Hertford O'Donnell he was entitled to write, M.R.C.S., for he had studied hard to gain this distinction, and the older surgeons at Guy's (his hospital) considered him one of the most rising operators of the day.

Having said chloroform was unknown at the time this story opens, it will strike my readers that, if Hertford O'Donnell were a rising and successful operator in those days, of necessity he combined within himself a larger number of striking qualities than are by any means necessary to form a successful operator in these.

There was more than mere hand skill, more than even thorough knowledge of his profession, then needful for the man, who, dealing with conscious subjects, essayed to rid them of some of the diseases to which flesh is heir. There was greater courage required in the manipulator of old than is altogether essential at present. Then, as now, a thorough mastery of his instruments, a steady hand, a keen eye, a quick dexterity were indispensable to a good operator; but, added to all these things, there formerly required a pulse which knew no quickening, a mental strength which never faltered, a ready power of adaptation in unexpected circumstances, fertility of resource in difficult cases, and a brave front under all emergencies.

If I refrain from adding that a hard as well as a courageous heart was an important item in the programme, it is only out of deference to general opinion, which, amongst other strange delusions, clings to the belief that courage and hardness are antagonistic qualities.

Hertford O'Donnell, however, was hard as steel. He understood his work, and he did it thoroughly; but he cared no more for quivering nerves and shrinking muscles, for screams of agony, for faces white with pain, and teeth clenched in the extremity of anguish, than he did for the stony countenances of the dead, which so often in the dissecting room appalled younger and less experienced men.

He had no sentiment, and he had no sympathy. The human body was to him, merely an ingenious piece of mechanism, which it was at once a pleasure and a profit to understand. Precisely as Brunel loved the Thames Tunnel, or any other singular engineering feat, so O'Donnell loved a patient on whom he had operated successfully, more especially if the ailment possessed by the patient were of a rare and difficult character.

And for this reason he was much liked by all who came under his hands, since patients are apt to mistake a surgeon's interest in their cases for interest in themselves; and it was gratifying to John Dicks, plasterer, and Timothy Regan, labourer, to be the happy possessors of remarkable diseases, which produced a cordial understanding between them and the handsome Irishman.

If he had been hard and cool at the moment of hacking them to pieces, that was all forgotten or remembered only as a virtue, when, after being discharged from hospital like soldiers who have served in a severe campaign, they met Mr. O'Donnell in the street, and were accosted by that rising individual just as though he considered himself nobody.

He had a royal memory, this stranger in a strange land, both for faces and cases; and like the rest of his countrymen, he never felt it beneath his dignity to talk cordially to corduroy and fustian.

In London, as at Calgillan, he never held back his tongue from speaking a cheery or a kindly word. His manners were pliable enough, if his heart were not; and the porters, and the patients, and the nurses, and the students at Guy's were all pleased to see Hertford O'Donnell.

Rain, hail, sunshine, it was all the same; there was a life and a brightness about the man which communicated itself to those with whom he came in contact. Let the mud in the Borough be a foot deep or the London fog as thick as pea-soup, Mr. O'Donnell never lost his temper, never muttered a surly reply to the gate-keeper's salutation, but spoke out blithely and cheerfully to his pupils and his patients, to the sick and to the well, to those below and to those above him.

And yet, spite of all these good qualities, spite of his handsome face, his fine figure, his easy address, and his unquestionable skill as an operator, the dons, who acknowledged his talent, shook their heads gravely when two or three of them in private and solemn conclave, talked confidentially of their younger brother.

If there were many things in his favour, there were more in his disfavour. He was Irish—not merely by the accident of birth, which might have been forgiven, since a man cannot be held accountable for such caprices of Nature, but by every other accident and design which is objectionable to the orthodox and respectable and representative English mind.

In speech, appearance, manner, taste, modes of expression, habits of life, Hertford O'Donnell was Irish. To the core of his heart he loved the island which he declared he never meant to re-visit; and amongst the English he moved to all intents and purposes a foreigner, who was resolved, so said the great prophets at Guy's, to rush to destruction as fast as he could, and let no man hinder him.

'He means to go the whole length of his tether,' observed one of the ancient wiseacres to another; which speech implied a conviction that Hertford O'Donnell having sold himself to the Evil One, had determined to dive the full length of his rope into wickedness before being pulled to that shore where even wickedness is negative—where there are no mad carouses, no wild, sinful excitements, nothing but impotent wailing and gnashing of teeth.

A reckless, graceless, clever, wicked devil—going to his natural home as fast as in London anyone possibly speed thither; this was the opinion his superiors, held of the man who lived all alone with a housekeeper and her husband (who acted as butler) in his big house near Soho.

Gerrard Street—made famous by De Quincey, was not then an utterly shady and forgotten locality; carriage-patients found their way to the rising young surgeon—some great personages thought it not beneath them to fee an individual whose consulting rooms were situated on what was even then considered the wrong side of Regent Street. He was making money, and he was spending it; he was over head and ears in debt—useless, vulgar debt—senselessly contracted, never bravely faced. He had lived at an awful pace ever since he came to London, a pace which only a man who hopes and expects to die young can ever travel.

Life, what good was it? Death, was he a child, or a woman, or a coward, to be afraid of that hereafter? God knew all about the trifle which had upset his coach, better than the dons at Guy's.

Hertford O'Donnell understood the world pretty thoroughly, and the ways thereof were to him as roads often traversed; therefore, when he said that at the Day of Judgment he felt certain he should come off as well as many of those who censured him, it may be assumed, that, although his views of post-mortem punishment were vague, unsatisfactory and infidel, still his information as to the peccadilloes of his neighbours was such as consoled himself.

And yet, living all alone in the old house near Soho Square, grave thoughts would intrude into the surgeon's mind—thoughts which were, so to say, italicised by peremptory letters, and still more peremptory visits from people who wanted money.

Although he had many acquaintances he had no single friend, and accordingly these thoughts were received and brooded over in solitude—in those hours when, after returning from dinner, or supper, or congenial carouse, he sat in his dreary rooms, smoking his pipe and considering means and ways, chances and certainties.

In good truth he had started in London with some vague idea that as his life in it would not be of long continuance, the pace at which he elected to travel could be of little consequence; but the years since his first entry into the Metropolis were now piled one on the top of another, his youth was behind him, his chances of longevity, spite of the way he had striven to injure his constitution, quite as good as ever. He had come to that period in existence, to that narrow strip of tableland, whence the ascent of youth and the descent of age are equally discernible—when, simply because he has lived for so many years, it strikes a man as possible he may have to live for just as many more, with the ability for hard work gone, with the boom companions scattered, with the capacity for enjoying convivial meetings a mere memory, with small means perhaps, with no bright hopes, with the pomp and the circumstance and the fairy carriages, and the glamour which youth flings over earthly objects, faded away like the pageant of yesterday, while the dreary ceremony of living has to be gone through today and tomorrow and the morrow after, as though the gay cavalcade and the martial music, and the glittering helmets and the prancing steeds were still accompanying the wayfarer to his journey's end.

Ah! my friends, there comes a moment when we must all leave the coach, with its four bright bays, its pleasant outside freight, its cheery company, its guard who blows the horn so merrily through villages and along lonely country roads.

Long before we reach that final stage, where the black business claims us for its own special property, we have to bid goodbye to all easy, thoughtless journeying, and betake ourselves, with what zest we may, to traversing the common of reality. There is no royal road across it that ever I heard of. From the king on his throne to the labourer who vaguely imagines what manner of being a king is, we have all to tramp across that desert at one period of our lives, at all events; and that period usually is when, as I have said, a man starts to find the hopes, and the strength, and the buoyancy of youth left behind, while years and years of life lie stretching out before him.

The coach he has travelled by drops him here. There is no appeal, there is no help; therefore, let him take off his hat and wish the new passengers good speed, without either envy or repining.

Behold, he has had his turn, and let whosoever will, mount on the box-seat of life again, and tip the coachman and handle the ribbons—he shall take that pleasant journey no more, no more for ever.

Even supposing a man's springtime to have been a cold and ungenial one, with bitter easterly winds and nipping frosts, biting the buds and retarding the blossoms, still it was spring for all that —spring with the young green leaves sprouting forth, with the flowers unfolding tenderly, with the songs of the birds and the rush of waters, with the summer before and the autumn afar off, and winter remote as death and eternity, but when once the trees have donned their summer foliage, when the pure white blossoms have disappeared, and the gorgeous red and orange and purple blaze of many-coloured flowers fills the gardens, then if there come a wet, dreary day, the idea of autumn and winter is not so difficult to realise. When once twelve o'clock is reached, the evening and night become facts, not possibilities; and it was of the afternoon, and the evening, and the night, Hertford O'Donnell sat thinking on the Christmas Eve, when I crave permission to introduce him to my readers.

A good-looking man ladies considered him. A tall, dark-complexioned, black-haired, straight-limbed, deeply divinely blue-eyed fellow, with a soft voice, with a pleasant brogue, who had ridden like a centaur over the loose stone walls in Connemara, who had danced all night at the Dublin balls, who had walked across the Bennebeola Mountains, gun in hand, day after day, without weariness, who had fished in every one of the hundred lakes you can behold from the top of that mountain near the Recess Hotel, who had led a mad, wild life in Trinity College, and a wilder, perhaps, while 'studying for a doctor'—as the Irish phrase goes—in Edinburgh, and who, after the death of his eldest brother left him free to return to Calgillan, and pursue the usual utterly useless, utterly purposeless, utterly pleasant life of an Irish gentleman possessed of health, birth, and expectations, suddenly kicked over the paternal traces, bade adieu to Calgillan Castle and the blandishments of a certain beautiful Miss Clifden, beloved of his mother, and laid out to be his wife, walked down the avenue without even so much company as a Gossoon to carry his carpet-bag, shook the dust from his feet at the lodge gates, and took his seat on the coach, never once looking back at Calgillan, where his favourite mare was standing in the stable, his greyhounds chasing one another round the home paddock, his gun at half-cock in his dressing-room and his fishing-tackle all in order and ready for use.

He had not kissed his mother, or asked for his father's blessing; he left Miss Clifden, arrayed in her brand-new riding-habit, without a word of affection or regret; he had spoken no syllable of farewell to any servant about the place; only when the old woman at the lodge bade him good morning and God-blessed his handsome face, he recommended her bitterly to look at it well for she would never see it more.

Twelve years and a half had passed since then, without either Miss Clifden or any other one of the Calgillan people having set eyes on Master Hertford's handsome face.

He had kept his vow to himself; he had not written home; he had not been indebted to mother or father for even a tenpenny-piece during the whole of that time; he had lived without friends;

and he had lived without God—so far as God ever lets a man live without him.

One thing only he felt to be needful—money; money to keep him when the evil days of sickness, or age, or loss of practice came upon him. Though a spendthrift, he was not a simpleton; around him he saw men, who, having started with fairer prospects than his own, were, nevertheless, reduced to indigence; and he knew that what had happened to others might happen to himself.

An unlucky cut, slipping on a piece of orange-peel in the street, the merest accident imaginable, is sufficient to change opulence to beggary in the life's programme of an individual, whose income depends on eye, on nerve, on hand; and, besides the consciousness of this fact, Hertford O'Donnell knew that beyond a certain point in his profession, progress was not easy.

It did not depend quite on the strength of his own bow and shield whether he counted his earnings by hundreds or thousands. Work may achieve competence; but mere work cannot, in a profession, at all events, compass fortune.

He looked around him, and he perceived that the majority of great men—great and wealthy—had been indebted for their elevation, more to the accident of birth, patronage, connection, or marriage, than to personal ability.

Personal ability, no doubt, they possessed; but then, little Jones, who lived in Frith Street, and who could barely keep himself and his wife and family, had ability, too, only he lacked the concomitants of success.

He wanted something or someone to puff him into notoriety—a brother at Court—a lord's leg to mend—a rich wife to give him prestige in Society; and in the absence of this something or someone, he had grown grey-haired and faint-hearted while labouring for a world which utterly despises its most obsequious servants.

'Clatter along the streets with a pair of fine horses, snub the middle classes, and drive over the commonalty—that is the way to compass wealth and popularity in England,' said Hertford O'Donnell, bitterly; and as the man desired wealth and popularity, he sat before his fire, with a foot on each hob, and a short pipe in his mouth, considering how he might best obtain the means to clatter along the streets in his carriage, and splash plebeians with mud from his wheels like the best.

In Dublin he could, by means of his name and connection, have done well; but then he was not in Dublin, neither did he want to be. The bitterest memories of his life were inseparable from the very name of the Green Island, and he had no desire to return to it.

Besides, in Dublin, heiresses are not quite so plentiful as in London; and an heiress, Hertford O'Donnell had decided, would do more for him than years of steady work.

A rich wife could clear him of debt, introduce him to fashionable practice, afford him that measure of social respectability which a medical bachelor invariably lacks, deliver him from the loneliness of Gerrard Street, and the domination of Mr. and Mrs. Coles.

To most men, deliberately bartering away their independence for money seems so prosaic a business that they strive to gloss it over even to themselves, and to assign every reason for their choice, save that which is really the influencing one.

Not so, however, with Hertford O'Donnell. He sat beside the fire scoffing over his proposed bargain—thinking of the lady's age, her money bags, her desirable house in town, her seat in the country, her snobbishness, her folly.

'It would be a fitting ending,' he sneered, 'and why I did not settle the matter tonight passes my comprehension. I am not a fool, to be frightened with old women's tales; and yet I must have turned white. I felt I did, and she asked me whether I were ill. And then to think of my being such an idiot as to ask her if she had heard anything like a cry, as though she would be likely to hear *that*, she with her poor parvenu blood, which I often imagine must have been mixed with some of her father's strong pickling vinegar. What the deuce could I have been dreaming about? I wonder what it really was.' And Hertford O'Donnell pushed his hair back off his forehead, and took another draught from the too familiar tumbler, which was placed conveniently on the chimney-piece.

63

'After expressly making up my mind to propose, too!' he mentally continued. 'Could it have been conscience—that myth, which somebody, who knew nothing about the matter, said, "Makes cowards of us all"? I don't believe in conscience; and even if there be such a thing capable of being developed by sentiment and cultivation, why should it trouble me? I have no intention of wronging Miss Janet Price Ingot, not the least. Honestly and fairly I shall marry her; honestly and fairly I shall act by her. An old wife is not exactly an ornamental article of furniture in a man's house; and I do not know that the fact of her being well gilded makes her look any handsomer. But she shall have no cause for complaint; and I will go and dine with her tomorrow, and settle the matter.'

Having arrived at which resolution, Mr. O'Donnell arose, kicked down the fire—burning hollow—with the heel of his boot, knocked the ashes out of his pipe, emptied his tumbler, and bethought him it was time to go to bed. He was not in the habit of taking his rest so early as a quarter to twelve o'clock; but he felt unusually weary —tired mentally and bodily—and lonely beyond all power of expression.

'The fair Janet would be better than this,' he said, half aloud; and then, with a start and a shiver, and a blanched face, he turned sharply round, whilst a low, sobbing, wailing cry echoed mournfully through the room. No form of words could give an idea of the sound. The plaintiveness of the Æolian harp—that plaintiveness which so soon affects and lowers the highest spirits—would have seemed wildly gay in comparison with the sadness of the cry which seemed floating in the air. As the summer wind comes and goes amongst the trees, so that mournful wail came and went—came and went. It came in a rush of sound, like a gradual crescendo managed by a skilful musician, and died away in a lingering note, so gently that the listener could scarcely tell the exact moment when it faded into utter silence.

I say faded, for it disappeared as the coast line disappears in the twilight, and there was total stillness in the apartment.

Then, for the first time, Hertford O'Donnell looked at his dog, and beholding the creature crouched into a corner beside the fire-place, called upon him to come out.

His voice sounded strange even to himself, and apparently the dog thought so too, for he made no effort to obey the summons.

'Come here, sir,' his master repeated, and then the animal came crawling reluctantly forward with his hair on end, his eyes almost starting from his head, trembling violently, as the surgeon, who caressed him, felt.

'So you heard it, Brian?' he said to the dog. 'And so your ears are sharper than Miss Ingot's, old fellow. It's a mighty queer thing to think of, being favoured with a visit from a Banshee in Gerrard Street; and as the lady has travelled so far, I only wish I knew whether there is any sort of refreshment she would like to take after her long journey.'

He spoke loudly, and with a certain mocking defiance, seeming to think the phantom he addressed would reply; but when he stopped at the end of his sentence, no sound came through the stillness. There was a dead silence in the room—a silence broken only by the falling of the cinders on the hearth and the breathing of his dog.

'If my visitor would tell me,' he proceeded, 'for whom this lamentation is being made, whether for myself, or for some member of my illustrious family, I should feel immensely obliged. It seems too much honour for a poor surgeon to have such attention paid him. Good Heavens! What is that?' he exlaimed, as a ring, loud and peremptory, woke all the echoes in the house, and brought his housekeeper, in a state of distressing dishabille, 'out of her warm bed', as she subsequently stated, to the head of the staircase.

Across the hall Hertford O'Donnell strode, relieved at the pros-pect of speaking to any living being. He took no precaution of putting up the chain, but flung the door wide. A dozen burglars would have proved welcome in comparison with that ghostly intruder he had been interviewing; therefore, as has been said, he threw the door wide, admitting a rush of wet, cold air, which made poor Mrs. Coles' few remaining teeth chatter in her head.

'Who is there? What do you want?' asked the surgeon, seeing

no person, and hearing no voice. 'Who is there? Why the devil can't you speak?'

When even this polite exhortation failed to elicit an answer, he passed out into the night and looked up the street and down the street, to see nothing but the driving rain and the blinking lights.

'If this goes on much longer I shall soon think I must be either mad or drunk,' he muttered, as he re-entered the house and locked and bolted the door once more.

'Lord's sake! What is the matter, sir?' asked Mrs. Coles, from the upper flight, careful only to reveal the borders of her night-cap to Mr. O'Donnell's admiring gaze. 'Is anybody killed? Have you to go out, sir?'

'It was only a run-away ring,' he answered, trying to reassure himself with an explanation he did not in his heart believe.

'Run-away—I'd run away them!' murmured Mrs. Coles, as she retired to the conjugal couch, where Coles was, to quote her own expression, 'snoring like a pig through it all'.

Almost immediately afterwards she heard her master ascend the stairs and close his bedroom door.

'Madam will surely be too much of a gentlewoman to intrude here,' thought the surgeon, scoffing even at his own fears; but when he lay down he did not put out his light, and made Brian leap up and crouch on the coverlet beside him.

The man was fairly frightened, and would have thought it no discredit to his manhood to acknowledge as much. He was not afraid of death, he was not afraid of trouble, he was not afraid of danger; but he was afraid of the Banshee; and as he laid with his hand on the dog's head, he recalled the many stories he had been told concerning this family retainer in the days of his youth.

He had not thought about her for years and years. Never before had he heard her voice himself. When his brother died she had not thought it necessary to travel up to Dublin and give him notice of the impending catastrophe. 'If she had, I would have gone down to Calgillan, and perhaps saved his life,' considered the surgeon. 'I wonder who this is for? If for me, that will settle my debts and my marriage. If I could be quite certain it was either of the old people, I would start tomorrow.'

Then vaguely his mind wandered on to think of every Banshee story he had ever heard in his life. About the beautiful lady with the wreath of flowers, who sat on the rocks below Red Castle, in the County Antrim, crying till one of the sons died for love of her; about the Round Chamber at Dunluce, which was swept clean by the Banshee every night; about the bed in a certain great house in Ireland, which was slept in constantly, although no human being ever passed in or out after dark; about that General Officer who, the night before Waterloo, said to a friend, 'I have heard the Banshee, and shall not come off the field alive tomorrow; break the news gently to poor Carry'; and who, nevertheless, coming safe off the field, had subsequently news about poor Carry broken tenderly and pitifully to him; about the lad, who, aloft in the rigging, hearing through the night a sobbing and wailing coming over the waters, went down to the captain and told him he was afraid they were somehow out of their reckoning, just in time to save the ship, which, when morning broke, they found but for his warning would have been on the rocks. It was blowing great guns, and the sea was all in a fret and turmoil, and they could sometimes see in the trough of the waves, as down a valley, the cruel black reefs they had escaped.

On deck the captain stood speaking to the boy who had saved them, and asking how he knew of their danger; and when the lad told him, the captain laughed, and said her ladyship had been outwitted that time.

But the boy answered, with a grave shake of his head, that the warning was either for him or his, and that if he got safe to port there would be bad tidings waiting for him from home; whereupon the captain bade him go below, and get some brandy and lie down.

He got the brandy, and he lay down, but he never rose again; and when the storm abated—when a great calm succeeded to the previous tempest—there was a very solemn funeral at sea; and on their arrival at Liverpool the captain took a journey to Ireland to tell a widowed mother how her only son died, and to bear his few effects to the poor desolate soul.

And Hertford O'Donnell thought again about his own father riding full-chase across country, and hearing, as he galloped by a clump of plantation, something like a sobbing and wailing. The hounds were in full cry, but he still felt, as he afterwards expressed it, that there was something among those trees he could not pass; and so he jumped off his horse, and hung the reins over the branch of a Scotch fir, and beat the cover well, but not a thing could he find in it.

Then, for the first time in his life, Miles O'Donnell turned his horse's head *from* the hunt, and, within a mile of Calgillan, met a man running to tell him his brother's gun had burst, and injured him mortally.

And he remembered the story also, of how Mary O'Donnell, his great aunt, being married to a young Englishman, heard the Banshee as she sat one evening waiting for his return; and of how she, thinking the bridge by which he often came home unsafe for horse and man, went out in a great panic, to meet and entreat him to go round by the main road for her sake. Sir Everard was riding along in the moonlight, making straight for the bridge, when he beheld a figure dressed all in white crossing it. Then there was a crash, and the figure disappeared.

The lady was rescued and brought back to the hall; but next morning there were two dead bodies within its walls—those of Lady Eyreton and her still-born son.

Quicker than I write them, these memories chased one another through Hertford O'Donnell's brain; and there was one more terrible memory than any, which would recur to him, concerning an Irish nobleman who, seated alone in his great town-house in London, heard the Banshee, and rushed out to get rid of the phantom, which wailed in his ear, nevertheless, as he strode down Piccadilly. And then the surgeon remembered how that nobleman went with a friend to the Opera, feeling sure that there no Banshee, unless she had a box, could find admittance, until suddenly he heard her singing up amongst the highest part of the scenery, with a terrible mournfulness, and a pathos which made the prima donna's tenderest notes seem harsh by comparison.

As he came out, some quarrel arose between him and a famous fire-eater, against whom he stumbled; and the result was that the next afternoon there was a new Lord —— vice Lord ——, killed in a duel with Captain Bravo.

Memories like these are not the most enlivening possible; they are apt to make a man fanciful, and nervous, and wakeful; but as time ran on, Hertford O'Donnell fell asleep, with his candle still burning, and Brian's cold nose pressed against his hand.

He dreamt of his mother's family—the Hertfords of Artingbury, Yorkshire, far-off relatives of Lord Hertford—so far off that even Mrs. O'Donnell held no clue to the genealogical maze.

He thought he was at Artingbury, fishing; that it was a misty summer morning, and the fish rising beautifully. In his dreams he hooked one after another, and the boy who was with him threw them into the basket.

At last there was one more difficult to land than the others; and the boy, in his eagerness to watch the sport, drew nearer and nearer to the brink, while the fisher, intent on his prey, failed to notice his companion's danger.

Suddenly there was a cry, a splash, and the boy disappeared from sight.

Next instant he rose again, however, and then, for the first time, Hertford O'Donnell saw his face.

It was one he knew well.

In a moment he plunged into the water, and struck out for the lad. He had him by the hair, he was turning to bring him back to land, when the stream suddenly changed into a wide, wild, shoreless sea, where the billows were chasing one another with a mad demoniac mirth.

For a while O'Donnell kept the lad and himself afloat. They were swept under the waves, and came up again, only to see larger waves rushing towards them; but through all, the surgeon never loosened his hold, until a tremendous billow, engulfing them both, tore the boy from his grasp.

With the horror of his dream upon him he awoke, to hear a voice quite distinctly:

'Go to the hospital—go at once!'

The surgeon started up in bed, rubbed his eyes, and looked around. The candle was flickering faintly in its socket. Brian, with his ears pricked forward, had raised his head at his master's sudden movement.

Everything was quiet, but still those words were ringing in his ear:

'Go to the hospital—go at once!'

The tremendous peal of the bell over night, and this sentence, seemed to be simultaneous.

That he was wanted at Guy's—wanted imperatively—came to O'Donnell like an inspiration. Neither sense nor reason had anything to do with the conviction that roused him out of bed, and made him dress as speedily as possible, and grope his way down the staircase, Brian following.

He opened the front door, and passed out into the darkness. The rain was over, and the stars were shining as he pursued his way down Newport Market, and thence, winding in and out in a south-easterly direction, through Lincoln's Inn Fields and Old Square to Chancery Lane, whence he proceeded to St. Paul's.

Along the deserted streets he resolutely continued his walk. He did not know what he was going to Guy's for. Some instinct was urging him on, and he neither strove to combat nor control it. Only once did the thought of turning back cross his mind, and that was at the archway leading into Old Square. There he had paused for a moment, asking himself whether he were not gone stark, staring mad; but Guy's seemed preferable to the haunted house in Gerrard Street, and he walked resolutely on, determined to say, if any surprise were expressed at his appearance, that he had been sent for.

Sent for?—yea, truly; but by whom?

On through Cannon Street; on over London Bridge, where the lights flickered in the river, and the sullen splash of the water flowing beneath the arches, washing the stone piers, could be heard, now the human din was hushed and lulled to sleep. On, thinking of many things: of the days of his youth; of his dead brother; of his father's heavily-encumbered estate; of the fortune his mother had vowed she would leave to some charity rather than to him, if he refused to marry according to her choice; of his wild life in London; of the terrible cry he had heard over-night—that unearthly wail which he could not drive from his memory even when he entered Guy's, and confronted the porter, who said:

'You have been sent for, sir; did you meet the messenger?'

Like one in a dream, Hertford O'Donnell heard him; like one in a dream, also, he asked what was the matter.

'Bad accident, sir; fire; fell off a balcony—unsafe—old building. Mother and child—a son; child with compound fracture of thigh.'

This, the joint information of porter and house-surgeon, mingled together, and made a boom in Mr. O'Donnell's ears like the sound of the sea breaking on a shingly shore.

Only one sentence he understood properly—'Immediate amputation necessary.' At this point he grew cool; he was the careful, cautious, successful surgeon, in a moment.

'The child you say?' he answered. 'Let me see him.'

The Guy's Hospital of today may be different to the Guy's Hertford O'Donnell knew so well. Railways have, I believe, swept away the old operating room; railways may have changed the position of the former accident ward, to reach which, in the days of which I am writing, the two surgeons had to pass a staircase leading to the upper stories.

On the lower step of this staircase, partially in shadow, Hertford O'Donnell beheld, as he came forward, an old woman seated.

An old woman with streaming grey hair, with attenuated arms, with head bowed forward, with scanty clothing, with bare feet; who never looked up at their approach, but sat unnoticing, shaking her head and wringing her hands in an extremity of despair.

'Who is that?' asked Mr. O'Donnell, almost involuntarily.

'Who is what?' demanded his companion.

'That—that woman,' was the reply.

'What woman?'

'There—are you blind?—seated on the bottom step of the staircase. What is she doing?' persisted Mr. O'Donnell.

'There is no woman near us,' his companion answered, looking at the rising surgeon very much as though he suspected him of seeing double.

'No woman!' scoffed Hertford. 'Do you expect me to disbelieve the evidence of my own eyes?' and he walked up to the figure, meaning to touch it.

But as he essayed to do so, the woman seemed to rise in the air and float away, with her arms stretched high up over her head, uttering such a wail of pain, and agony, and distress, as caused the Irishman's blood to curdle.

'My God! Did you hear that?' he said to his companion.

'What?' was the reply.

Then, although he knew the sound had fallen on deaf ears, he answered:

'The wail of the Banshee! Some of my people are doomed!'

'I trust not,' answered the house-surgeon, who had an idea, nevertheless, that Hertford O'Donnell's Banshee lived in a whisky bottle, and would at some not remote day make an end of the rising and clever operator.

With nerves utterly shaken, Mr. O'Donnell walked forward to the accident ward. There with his face shaded from the light, lay his patient—a young boy, with a compound fracture of the thigh.

In that ward, in the face of actual danger or pain capable of relief the surgeon had never known faltering or fear; and now he carefully examined the injury, felt the pulse, inquired as to the treatment pursued, and ordered the sufferer to be carried to the operating room.

While he was looking out his instruments he heard the boy lying on the table murmur faintly:

'Tell her not to cry so—tell her not to cry.'

'What is he talking about?' Hertford O'Donnell inquired.

'The nurse says he has been speaking about some woman crying ever since he came in—his mother, most likely,' answered one of the attendants.

'He is delirious then?' observed the surgeon.

'No, sir,' pleaded the boy, excitedly, 'no; it is that woman—that woman with the grey hair. I saw her looking from the upper window before the balcony gave way. She has never left me since, and she won't be quiet, wringing her hands and crying.'

'Can you see her now?' Hertford O'Donnell inquired, stepping to the side of the table. 'Point out where she is.'

Then the lad stretched forth a feeble finger in the direction of the door, where clearly, as he had seen her seated on the stairs, the surgeon saw a woman standing—a woman with grey hair and scanty clothing, and upstretched arms and bare feet.

'A word with you, sir,' O'Donnell said to the house-surgeon, drawing him back from the table. 'I cannot perform this operation: send for some other person. I am ill; I am incapable.'

'But,' pleaded the other, 'there is no time to get anyone else. We sent for Mr. West, before we troubled you, but he was out of town, and all the rest of the surgeons live so far away. Mortification may set in at any moment, and—'

'Do you think you require to teach me my business?' was the reply. 'I know the boy's life hangs on a thread, and that is the very reason I cannot operate. I am not fit for it. I tell you I have seen tonight that which unnerves me utterly. My hand is not steady. Send for someone else without delay. Say I am ill—dead!—what you please. Heavens! There she is again, right over the boy! Do you hear her?' and Hertford O'Donnell fell fainting on the floor.

How long he lay in that death-like swoon I cannot say; but when he returned to consciousness, the principal physician of Guy's was standing beside him in the cold grey light of the Christmas morning.

'The boy?' murmured O'Donnell, faintly.

'Now, my dear fellow, keep yourself quiet,' was the reply.

'The boy?' he repeated, irritably. 'Who operated?'

'No one,' Dr. Lanson answered. "It would have been useless cruelty. Mortification had set in, and—'

Hertford O'Donnell turned his face to the wall, and his friend could not see it.

'Do not distress yourself,' went on the physician, kindly. 'Allington says he could not have survived the operation in any case. He was quite delirious from the first, raving about a woman with grey hair and—'

'I know,' Hertford O'Donnell interrupted; 'and the boy had a mother, they told me, or I dreamt it.'

'Yes, she was bruised and shaken, but not seriously injured.'

'Has she blue eyes and fair hair—fair hair all rippling and wavy? Is she white as a lily, with just a faint flush of colour in her cheek? Is she young and trusting and innocent? No; I am wandering. She must be nearly thirty now. Go, for God's sake, and tell me if you can find a woman you could imagine having once been as a girl such as I describe.'

'Irish?' asked the doctor; and O'Donnell made a gesture of assent.

'It is she then,' was the reply; 'a woman with the face of an angel.'

'A woman who should have been my wife,' the surgeon answered; 'whose child was my son.'

'Lord help you!' ejaculated the doctor. Then Hertford O'Donnell raised himself from the sofa where they had laid him, and told his companion the story of his life—how there had been bitter feud between his people and her people—how they were divided by old animosities and by difference of religion—how they had met by stealth, and exchanged rings and vows, all for naught—how his family had insulted hers, so that her father, wishful for her to marry a kinsman of his own, bore her off to a far-away land, and made her write him a letter of eternal farewell—how his own parents had kept all knowledge of the quarrel from him till she was utterly beyond his reach—how they had vowed to discard him unless he agreed to marry according to their wishes—how he left his home, and came to London, and sought his fortune. All this Hertford O'Donnell repeated; and when he had finished, the bells were ringing for morning service—ringing loudly, ringing joyfully, 'Peace on earth, goodwill towards men'.

But there was little peace that morning for Hertford O'Donnell. He had to look on the face of his dead son, wherein he beheld, as though reflected, the face of the boy in his dream.

Afterwards, stealthily he followed his friend, and beheld, with her eyes closed, her cheeks pale and pinched, her hair thinner but still falling like a veil over her, the love of his youth, the only woman he had ever loved devotedly and unselfishly.

There is little space left here to tell of how the two met at last —of how the stone of the years seemed suddenly rolled away from the tomb of their past, and their youth arose and returned to them, even amid their tears.

She had been true to him, through persecution, through contumely, through kindness, which was more trying; through shame, and grief, and poverty, she had been loyal to the lover of her youth; and before the New Year dawned there came a letter from Calgillan, saying that the Banshee's wail had been heard there, and praying Hertford, if he were still alive, to let bygones be bygones, in consideration of the long years of estrangement—the anguish and remorse of his afflicted parents.

More than that. Hertford O'Donnell, if a reckless man, was honourable; and so, on the Christmas Day when he was to have proposed for Miss Ingot, he went to that lady, and told her how he had wooed and won, in the years of his youth, one who after many days was miraculously restored to him; and from the hour in which he took her into his confidence, he never thought her either vulgar or foolish, but rather he paid homage to the woman who, when she had heard the whole tale repeated, said, simply, 'Ask her to come to me till you can claim her—and God bless you both!'

CHARLOTTE RIDDELL

Charlotte Riddell was born in Carrickfergus, County Antrim, Ireland in 1832. In her late teens, in the space of just five years, both her parents died, and at the age of 25 she married Joseph Hadley Riddell, a civil engineer. Very little is known beyond this about Riddell's life, other than that she lived in London and was one of the most popular authors of the Victorian era, writing more than thirty novels and a good amount of short stories. She was also part-owner and editor of *St. James's Magazine*, one of the most prestigious literary magazines of the 1860s. Nowadays, her best-known work is probably her collection of ghost stories, *Weird Stories*, first published in 1882. She died of breast cancer in 1906 in Ashford, Kent, aged 75. Her obituary in *The Times* read "Mrs. Riddell always wrote carefully, displayed much insight into character, and skill in manipulating her materials. The tone of her novels was invariably wholesome."

www.ingramcontent.com/pod-product-compliance
Lightning Source LLC
Chambersburg PA
CBHW060406030726
47497CB00003B/870